LET THE GUNS DECIDE

Death comes to the little town of Macallister in the form of a milk-drinking, baby-faced killer who leaves bodies in the dust. Lone Lee Kirby rides into a town desperate for help, but the body count grows as Kirby is forced to face his own demons.

SHANE ARCHER

LET THE GUNS DECIDE

Complete and Unabridged

LINFORD
Leicester

First published in Great Britain in 2011 by
Robert Hale Limited
London

First Linford Edition
published 2013
by arrangement with
Robert Hale Limited
London

A catalogue record for this book is available
from the British Library.

ISBN 978–1–4448–1560–3

Published by
F. A. Thorpe (Publishing)
Anstey, Leicestershire

Set by Words & Graphics Ltd.
Anstey, Leicestershire
Printed and bound in Great Britain by
T. J. International Ltd., Padstow, Cornwall

This book is printed on acid-free paper

1

Mystery Town

Halfway between the Rogantown County borderline and the big railroad town to the east, the long trail dipped through a fertile valley to touch the little town of Macallister before hurrying on to more important places on the Colorado map.

The stage passed through just twice weekly, and most everyone who either embarked or disembarked at Race Thompson's stage depot was a local.

Strangers were rare in Macallister, and though they were treated in a friendly enough fashion they always had the feeling they were somehow intruding.

'We Macallisters keep purty much to ourselves here, I guess,' old greybearded Petrie might be heard remark when any stranger was within earshot. 'The outside world's got its ways and we got ours, and I guess the two never did mix nohow.'

Heads would nod at such wisdom, the stranger would take the hint and soon be on his way, leaving life in Macallister to drift along as before — sleepy, sun-soaked and maybe even a little on the dull side. Or at least that was how life could appear to an observer — the way it was always meant to look.

The reality of life in Macallister was in truth very different from the picture presented by its drowsy, cowtown appearance. That was Macallister's secret, and it was guarded well.

The day the trouble came began like any other in Macallister. The first citizen abroad was Doolin, the water carter, who harnessed his team to his rusted wagon and went rumbling off to Crow Creek to fill up with his first load of the day.

By around seven, with some of the towners still abed, Doolin's wagon would trundle along Trail Street, spraying water from rusted jets in the endless task of laying the summer's dust.

By the time Doolin was heading back to the Crow for the second load, Sheriff Coe Walters would be striding along Mount Street heading for his office, while Mayor Hinch puffed his first fat cigar of the day standing in the windows of his handsome home while waiting for the housemaid to call him to breakfast.

The water carter, the sheriff and the mayor had all been in Macallister a long time. Each man was solid, reliable, churchgoing and sober. And if they did display certain signs of affluence that might seem out of keeping with their respective trades, then it didn't seem all that remarkable. For the fact was that most everybody in this man's town appeared much better off than his counterpart someplace else.

So there were few critics or malcontents here, and what few there might be who from time to time were heard to query how come most everyone from the water carter up to the mayor himself seemed unworried by money troubles of any kind, the general run of citizens seemed simply not to notice . . .

The young stranger who rode in at nine o'clock that morning barely noticed the town or its solid air of prosperity at all. But the inhabitants certainly noticed *him*.

The horseman's pale-blue eyes appeared to touch every man, woman and child as he made his leisurely way along towards the central block. When it came to sizing up a place this man missed nothing, while in return the town continued to make a very long and vaguely uneasy appraisal of him.

'Guntoter,' old Petrie decided. He spat in the dust surrounding his bench beneath the peppercorn tree by the hotel. He nodded his head for emphasis. 'Yessir, that's his brand sure enough. Wonder what rock this 'un crawled out from under?'

4

Petrie's bunch saw a small, slightly pudgy rider in immaculate brown rig with soft blond hair gleaming from beneath a low-crowned brown Stetson. He sported a pair of big-handled Colts on his hips, yet didn't really appear dangerous somehow.

'Looks more like a cowboy of some kind to me,' another remarked. 'Well-heeled, but harmless enough, don't you reckon?'

'Ever see Billy the Kid?' old Petrie countered, knowing damn well he was the only man in town ever to have had that dubious experience.

'Here he goes on Billy the Kid again,' somebody scoffed from the adjoining balcony. 'Face like an angel . . . and what else did they say about Billy?' he taunted, prompting the oldster to come back.

'Face like an angel and eyes as blue as a Rocky Mountain sky,' Petrie declared. 'The kind of boy you'd take into your home without a second thought, a baby-faced feller of just

5

twenty-one who looked more like a choir-boy than the meanest, fastest and hell-bentest young gunslinger this world ever did see. That was Billy the Kid, mister. And I tell you, that stranger yonder looks enough like the Kid to be his cousin.'

The slim-hipped young Fabian might have been amused to hear himself compared to the boyish hero of every hot-gun hellion in the South-west. Amused, maybe, but far from flattered. For he believed himself to be faster, braver and meaner even than the late William Bonney of Lincoln County, New Mexico, ever knew how to be.

But old Petrie was right about the stranger's profession. Gunslinger he was, and it was the deadly business of the gun that brought him to this place on the first Monday of the new summer.

There were men in Macallister marked down for death.

★ ★ ★

It was a rare day indeed that there wasn't some kind of a wind blowing high up around the granite ledges of Buzzard Butte, the standout landmark for a hundred miles or more. The breeze was cooling the sultry morning down some following the rider's sweaty climb up to the lookout ledge — even though Moss O'Shea was not appreciating it much. It was threatening to snatch away his hard-hitter hat as he tried to focus his field glasses upon that distant blob of colour that was the town of Macallister.

'Damnation!' he cussed, clutching his hat with one hand and the glasses with the other. That was his strongest expletive. Moss O'Shea was a killer, thief and kidnapper, but the one vice he avoided was foul language. He'd made a promise to his mother on her deathbed that his tongue would forever remain pure. It was a mercy indeed that the old dear had not lived long enough to realize just what a back-shooting butcher she had bequeathed to an

already sinful world.

O'Shea's companion said nothing. He was younger than the outlaw, gun-barrel straight and youthfully muscled with a faint glint of humour showing in the depths of grey eyes. He appeared very hard, yet was not yet totally brutalized by the life he'd chosen. O'Shea, on the other hand, simply reflected the elemental toughness of his breed plus an added element of viciousness.

Upon first meeting Moss O'Shea, any man with the intelligence of an ape would smell the danger coming off him, and avoid him like the plague.

But the younger and slighter of this pair could have easily been mistaken for a simple wrangler, a ranch hand, or maybe something even a cut above, such as a coach guard.

Both wore tied-down six-shooters but that was where all similarity ended.

O'Shea had but recently recruited Lee Kirby into his maverick bunch because of his gunspeed, but whether

or not he would develop into topflight outlaw material was yet to be seen.

Kirby had been riding with the bunch for just a fortnight now and this was his first big job . . .

O'Shea was at last forced to remove his big hat and set it aside to enable him to work the glasses properly. The bald spot at the back of his head gleamed as he fixed the glasses upon distant Macallister. What this man lacked in youthful vigour he compensated for with natural cunning and a flinty nerve.

The binoculars magnified an unremarkable township with a main stem about a quarter-mile long bisected four times by cross streets. Stores, marshalling yards and dust. That was Macallister.

He grunted as he lowered the glasses to stand a while longer musing and tapping one foot. His companion showed no impatience, no emotion. Kirby had once been a professional Indian fighter. He knew how to wait, a talent which

9

many a man of his ilk had gone to his grave without ever mastering.

'Guess I dunno what I rightly expected,' O'Shea ventured at last. 'But I reckon whatever it was it had to be somethin' more'n this.' His gesture embraced the distant town. 'This looks just like every other one-horser and loser city between here and Denver, son. Mebbe we been given a bum steer?'

Kirby studied O'Shea without speaking, his eyes deep, blue and old in his youthful pan. He was thinking how much O'Shea resembled a suspicious-minded old honey bear, with his grizzled tufts of hair and a bulbous snout.

A hint of a smile eventually lightened his expression and that only made O'Shea sore.

'Somethin' funny, kid? Well, why don't you tell me so we can both have a laugh? I could use one right about now.'

Kirby schooled his features to blankness. 'Guess I never expected it to look just the same as any other hick town is all, boss.'

'Why so?'

'Well, if they're as clever and cunnin' as folks say . . . ' His voice trailed off as the other scowled.

'That's just one of the things that show their smarts, mister — ' O'Shea began, but broke off. He was a tetchy man by nature but didn't want to rile the other on account he had come to trust him, maybe even respected him some. He had hopes Kirby would make a reliable gun *segundo*; he could sure use one right about now.

He decided it was high time to put the other to the test. 'Kirby, I want you to mosey on down yonder.'

'Alone?'

'Yeah. Go spy her out. You know what to look for. Get the lie of the land, find out who's who and what's what. You ain't wanted anywhere hereabouts so nobody's gonna take one lick of notice of you. Me and the boys can rest up in the canyon while you're at it, and

11

that way we'll be good and fresh when the time comes to move in.'

Kirby raised no objections. Within the hour, he was pushing his bay saddler through the brushy region south of Bracken Canyon and heading for the creek which he planned to follow down to the town trail.

He'd always liked riding alone.

Ever since his folks had died on him during the Civil War, he'd been a loner. There had been several women and just a handful of men he'd ever called friend. But nothing or nobody ever held him long. He'd learned the truth of that old adage about 'rolling stones'. He'd 'gathered no moss' in his twenty-four years, had been down to his last dollar bill when arrested in the South on a bogus horse-stealing charge. While under arrest he'd met a drunk who rode with the notorious O'Shea bunch.

One thing led to another and soon he'd found himself riding with O'Shea and resolving to shake his hard-luck tag, once and for all.

So it was that a slightly reluctant yet determined gunman followed Crow Creek towards the same trail by which another lone stranger had reached Macallister several hours before.

* * *

'You want milk?' the barkeep asked suspiciously.

'Milk.'

The barkeep started to grin, then thought better of it. He'd been pulling beer and pouring whiskey in Macallister's Diamondback saloon a long time now and had developed a sixth sense regarding customers. This baby-faced man with the soft fair hair and pale-blue eyes had been loafing around town for some hours and was starting to make some folks edgy, the barkeep amongst them. Yet he obligingly poured the milk without comment and moved down the bar to wait on his regulars.

Fabian sipped his drink and met the curious eyes in the bar mirror with a smile. Hastily, they looked away, but not before he'd seen them. They were at once curious, suspicious and likely nervous, but tried not to let it show.

Several had already put to him several variations of the, 'Just passin' through, stranger?' line here in Macallister. His answer on each occasion was simply a smile and a vague shrug. They wanted him to leave, it was plain, but he was just beginning to settle in.

He adjusted the weight of his double gun-rig about his hips and listened to the conversation at a nearby table.

'So . . . I told Tad that if he couldn't get me one of them new wagons with the cut-under front gear by the end of the month, I'd just have to send away to Villanova for one. I want that there vehicle and I want it now.'

The speaker had the rugged face and barrel chest of a blacksmith. Yet he dressed in broadcloth and flashed a bulging billfold when he bought drinks. Macallister didn't look prosperous enough to sustain a blacksmith in comfort, much less style, but this citizen was plainly doing well.

As was one of his table companions, the bearded liveryman, Race Thompson.

'I'm takin' the family up to Villanova on vacation next week, Joe,' this one stated, fiddling with a fifty-cent cigar some before lighting up. 'I can place your order for you if you want?'

Voices faded into the background murmur as the gunfighter returned his attention to the mirror.

Most everybody around here seemed flush, he was thinking. Real flush.

Indeed, the longer he spent here the more convinced he became that Macallister was stinking rich. He also suspected he knew why it was so, and decided that 'The Plan' should be put into operation without further delay.

He drank and ordered another. He was at his best whenever the scent of blood was in the air and he would feel that old familiar tingling in his finger-tips. Everyday *hombres*, he was sure, never but never got to feel that magical excitement that came when emerging victorious from danger — and so were never more than half alive. He knew it was only by playing with death that a man ever got to experience *real* life.

His drink arrived just as the water carter showed. Doolin was a plain, blunt character who had never seen a full glass of milk standing upon the Diamondback's long bar before, and consequently appeared noticeably surprised as he tugged off his sweat-rimmed hat and bawled loudly for a beer — a man's drink.

'Hey, what's ailin' you, pard?' he grinned at the stranger, not at all offensively. 'Feelin' a little on the poorly side, are we?'

'Pardon?'

Fabian's tone was soft. Like his appearance. He appeared to be smiling as he turned his sleek head towards Doolin, but maybe that was just a trick of the light.

'The milk.'

'You got something against people drinking milk?'

Doolin blew the froth from his beer. 'Hell no, just remarkin'.' He hefted his tankard. 'Here's lookin' at you, stranger.'

'First, the apology.'

Fabian didn't appear to speak loudly, and yet everybody heard. The level of noise in the saloon ebbed as Doolin lowered his tankard, looking puzzled. 'Huh?'

'You were mocking me for drinking milk, mister. I can't let that go by.'

Doolin's honest, big-eared face reddened.

'Tarnation take it, stranger, I wasn't for mockin' you. Just passin' the time of day.'

'Then it won't hurt you to retract.'

'Retract?' Doolin slowly set his hefty glass down on the bartop. 'What's that mean?'

'Sorry, I'm forgetting that I'm talking with a thick-witted backwoods hick who likely never attended school. So, I'll make it as simple as I can.

Apologize, and we'll let it go at that.'

Mayor Hinch was at a corner table; the killer had made certain beforehand he was present. Predictably, the gentlemanly Hinch rose and approached to intercede on the water carrier's behalf.

'I'm afraid you're getting off your horse on the wrong side, stranger,' he said placatingly. 'I know this man through and through. He wouldn't give offence if you paid him. If he upset you in any way, you can take it from me that it was purely accidental.'

'In other words,' Fabian breathed, 'you're calling me a liar.'

The colour drained from the mayor's face. Hinch was a large man with meaty jowls and bushy eyebrows. He ran the hotel and largely the town itself. He was unaccustomed to being addressed in such a manner but, unlike Doolin, quickly realized this man might be dangerous.

'Nothing of the sort — ' he began, but Doolin cut him off.

'Dad-bust it, stranger, anybody with

half a brain could tell nobody's tryin' to insult you. You're just actin' up like a wild colt when the wind changes direction. Why don't you drink up your cow juice and just simmer down?'

Everyone seemed to reckon that a fine notion — with the exception of the fair-haired stranger with the secret cat smile and low-tied guns.

He moved away from the bar and let his hands hang down close to holstered Colts. He no longer appeared small or soft somehow. It was as if anger had suddenly hardened him and expanded him to a larger and more dangerous dimension.

He said, 'I've been insulted. Back where I hail from, a man only knows one way to answer an insult. So — who's drawin' first? Or maybe you'd like to whistle up some backin', pilgrim? Hell, go ahead if you've a mind, makes no never-mind to me.'

A deep silence had descended upon the Diamondback saloon as everybody realized that a truly dangerous situation

19

had arisen, yet plainly from nothing. Men attempted to be quiet and unobtrusive as they edged away from the contested area before the bar, yet every scrape of chair, every step, seemed magnified in this taut silence.

'You . . . you fixin' to throw down on us?' Doolin croaked disbelievingly.

'No, of course he's not, man,' Mayor Hinch said nervously.

'Wrong again,' Fabian stated. 'You could make a career out of being wrong every time, Mr Mayor.' He flexed his fingers and his eyes were chips of steel. 'Now . . . go for your shooters you big-mouthed, yellow-gutted sons of bitches. I'm claiming my satisfaction in blood!'

There was no chance Mayor Hinch would have drawn his Banker's Special had Doolin not come clear first. Doolin was treacle-slow, but in no way lacking in guts. His weapon cleared leather with a sibilant hiss and started upwards, and for one long second he looked just like a genuine gunfighter with his crouched stance and left arm spread wide for balance, the big Navy Colt shimmering in the light.

But only for a second.

Fabian appeared to shrug. Yet in the next instant there was a roaring .45 in his fist and Doolin went staggering backwards with leaden nails thudding into his chest. The water-carter struck the bar edge, half-turned, stopped another slug to the side of the head and fell dead without a cry.

The killer's smoking gun transcribed a brief arc to freeze upon Hinch, whose cutters were but halfway clear of the leather. The mayor froze when both pale-blue eyes and smoking weapon focused upon him. His face twisted into a mask of sheer horror and his lips moved with words nobody heard in the split-second before he too was gunned down.

Fabian pumped three slugs into the man's chest as he tumbled. He hadn't cared if he killed Doolin or not; the man was unimportant. But Hinch was one of the two names upon his list and had been doomed since the first moment Fabian rode into town.

Who would kill so mercilessly for such little cause?

Patrons were still gawping in disbelief when the batwings swung inwards and Sheriff Walters came in at the run — gun in fist.

Fabian swung smoothly to confront the peace officer, left hand palming his second Colt in one fluent movement. He raised the weapon to firing level in one smooth and unhurried motion. The gun was spewing hot lead before Walters's eyes were able to absorb the terrible scene. The gunslinger proved as murderously adept with the left hand as he was with the right.

A fusillade of bullets ripped into Walters's stocky body. The man didn't have a prayer in hell, yet somehow managed to get a single shot away into the ceiling before being slammed backwards into the batwings with brutal force. Desperately, like a drowning man, he reached out and broke a batwing clear of its hinges as he plummeted down to the floorboards. He fell on one side and rolled slowly over on to his back, the star upon his chest pattered with crimson as he breathed his last . . .

They were toting the dead men across Trail Street for the undertaker's when later that day the second stranger rode in from the direction of Crow Creek.

Nobody seemed to notice him.

It was years since anybody had died violently in Macallister, and nobody as yet seemed capable of digesting that grisly new reality. Yet the truth was that within the space of mere minutes three honest men had surrendered their lives, including the town's most prominent citizens, its mayor and sheriff.

It was a town in deep shock which Lee Kirby entered astride his long-legged bay horse.

2

Along Came Kirby

Kirby stood at the long cedar bar of Fat Libby's Saloon, his muscular back leaning against the counter, one boot hooked carelessly over the footrail of the piano with bony hands prancing up and down the keyboard while a pair of half-naked dancing girls high-kicked and sashayed up and down the little stage in the corner.

There were customers aplenty that night yet nobody applauded when their musical number came to a climax. This was understandable. It was less than two hours since murderous events had erupted at the Diamondback and many were still deep in shock.

To the eye of any observer it appeared that most of the town was still preoccupied with the shootings they'd seen, with nobody really interested in the entertainment.

The killer had not ridden out and the whole town was still jittery.

Yet Fat Libby was determined the show must go on. 'Let's have 'Oh! Susanna', Professor!' she bellowed from the stairway landing. 'And let's see some of you broken-winded cowboys get up offen your duffs and do a bit of stompin' and toe-tappin'. I ain't runnin' no wake here, you hear?'

Virtually everybody seemed to be out and about that night, not merely to kick up their heels and get rotten, as usual, but rather to get together and hash over recent violent events. Blood had been spilled right here in the saloon, the killer was still in town and the entire place was afraid. So, Fat Libby was bent upon reviving morale.

Yet there was but a half-hearted response to her leather-lunged bellow now, and it was only too plain their hearts weren't in it as a couple of cowhands twirled some flinty-faced percentage girls around the floor to the strains of 'Oh! Susanna'.

A pale girl in a low-cut blouse approached Kirby but was dismissed with a shake of the head. He wasn't here to dance, drink or raise any hell. He was working, even if he didn't look it as he leant back against the long bar nursing a soda water and a crooked black Mexican cigar.

Kirby watched the drinkers and they watched him. Although a different breed from the smooth-featured Fabian, he was still another stranger who wore his six-shooter low on the hip and moved just like a man who knew how to use it.

Macallister was jittery about any and every stranger this violent night, and Kirby was aware he'd been under constant surveillance ever since entering Fat Libby's following his rare-steak chow down at the eatery.

This didn't faze him. He expected nothing less in the wake of the day's brutal events.

He'd steered well clear of that cat-smirking gunslinger since his arrival, though nursing a strong suspicion that Fabian might be growing curious about him. Kirby, in return, was suspicious of Fabian's presence in the town, and had been genuinely sobered by the grisly sight of the three bloodied corpses at the funeral parlour.

Upon entering Macallister for the first time earlier, he hadn't anticipated such a sequence of bloody events. But if that was how the cards here were being dealt, then he had no option but to play them out however they might fall.

His attention drifted back to the group hunched around a corner table beneath a badly smoking oil lamp. The bartender had informed him that the bunch comprised Macallister's newsman, undertaker, stage-line operator and livery boss.

All four appeared prosperous, uneasy — and very much conscious of his presence.

As he glanced away he caught the tall

27

man with the ink-stained fingers staring across at him. On impulse, Kirby lifted his glass in the man's direction, causing him to flush and instantly turn away, just as the barman approached to wait on him.

Kirby said, 'Your friends over yonder look a bit jittery about me, boy. You got any notion why?'

'Guess we're edgy about most everybody tonight,' the man replied candidly. 'Wonderin' who'll be next, most likely.'

'Fabian still in town?'

'So I hear.' The man looked him over, his gaze lingering longest upon the .45 resting snugly in its tied-down and hand-tooled leather holster, riding his right thigh. 'Guess you ain't the jittery breed, though?'

'Why shouldn't I be?'

'I guess mainly on account that you look like a feller who can look after himself.'

Kirby glanced away, shifting the cigar from one side of his jaw to the other. Sure, he could look out for himself. In truth he was damned good at it. He could fight, shoot or wrestle with anybody and most always came out on top.

Yet at twenty-five years of age that didn't seem that much for a man to hang on to or boast about. Those things he could not do or had not been trained for seemed endless by comparison. He couldn't stay in one job or the same place for any length of time. Couldn't stay interested in one woman, couldn't boast more than one or two close friends he'd made in life thus far. He was a loner-drifter who'd eventually failed at most everything he'd ever attempted, until now finding himself trying out another new trade for the first time — outlawry.

He stared into his glass, suddenly wishing it was straight whiskey now. When he looked up, the newsman with the bushy hair and inky fingers was approaching.

''Evenin', young feller,' he was greeted. 'I'm Mitchell Craig from the

29

Macallister Courier.'

'Yeah, I know.'

'Mind if we talk some?'

'You're talkin', ain't you?'

'Why, I guess I am at that, Mister . . . Mister . . . ?'

'Lee.'

'Lee. Would that be your first name or the last?'

'It's my name if I say it is. Now, what do you want with me, newsman?'

Craig leaned an elbow on the bar. He was a lean-bodied man with quick and intelligent eyes. He didn't appear to be put off by Kirby's gruffness as he subjected him to a steady scrutiny.

'Reckon you'll know me next time?'

'I'm sorry,' the man said. 'Look, there likely isn't any polite way to come out with this, so I'll just ask you straight. Are you for hire? As a gunman, I mean?'

'What?'

Craig jerked a thumb in the direction of his table. 'We all came to the conclusion that you could be one and I

30

was elected to make the approach. You see, we feel we might require the services of a gun professional at any moment, for reasons I'm sure you can guess at.'

'You want me to kill Fabian?'

The newsman looked shocked. 'Hell, no! What we're looking for is simply somebody who can stand up to him on our behalf and persuade him to quit town before he murders someone else.'

'Same thing,' Kirby grunted. 'If I get to brace that gunslick thataway, powder could burn. You never get just to shift that breed on, Craig. They go whenever they want, or else they go feet first. There's no middle ground with Fabian's kind.'

'You speak like someone with experience of men like that.'

Kirby glanced away. He knew the fast gun type all right. Just as he knew the gamblers, the percenters, the frauds and the badmen and all the rest of that get-rich-quick ilk. He wasn't proud of this, that was just the way it was.

'You've got the wrong man, Craig,' he said woodenly. 'I'm just a drifter on my way through. I ain't interested in your town or your problems. But if you're looking for someone to take care of Fabian, why not the law?'

'The law is dead, man. Fabian shot it.'

'He shot the sheriff? Well, what about outside law?'

'The nearest law's in Villanova, eighty miles away. And even if they sent over a marshal, I don't know what he could do. Fabian merely defended himself.'

'So your only hope is for somebody to gun this man down?'

'I keep telling you we don't want that.'

'And I keep telling you it's what you do want, only you're too much a gent or too dumb to admit it.'

'I can see I'm wasting my time with you,' Craig said stiffly, drawing back. 'I won't trouble you further.'

But Kirby wasn't ready to let him go. A newsman could be a mine of information and he was hunting information right now.

So he followed the tall figure as he made for the door, calling after him as he went out.

'Hold up, Craig. Let me walk a ways with you . . . just in case you get jumped by some guntoter.'

Although plainly peeved, Craig did not reject his offer. Kirby could see the man was jittery as they started along the street. Maybe if he were honest with himself he'd admit he was just a little uneasy himself.

They walked as they talked, Kirby firing off questions and Craig answering readily enough. The queries were to do with Macallister and its sources of income, which the newsman listed as cattle, timber and sheep in that order.

He didn't mention mining, so Kirby did.

'Any gold or silver hereabouts, Craig?'

Craig almost succeeded in appearing casual as he answered. Almost . . .

'Not so much as a trace, Lee. What makes you ask?'

'Just curious.' Kirby put on one of his rare smiles. 'It sure beats working for a living, digging money out of the ground, don't it?'

'I suppose it does,' Craig responded vaguely as they rounded a corner. 'Here's where I live. Care to come in for coffee, Lee?'

'Some other time,' Kirby grunted in the same moment that he saw the girl standing in the doorway of the next house, young, fresh-faced and innocent-looking in a place where that kind was mighty scarce.

And he suddenly thought, 'How long is it since you spent time with a genuine lady, Kirby?' Forever, seemed the right answer.

And while he was staring they reached the stoop and Craig was introducing them. 'My daughter, Jade. Jade, this is my friend, Lee Kirby.'

The girl's lovely face turned cold. 'I know. The *other* gunman.'

This didn't seem promising, but Craig quickly stepped in, admonishing the girl and insisting she was judging his new friend unfairly.

'No harm done,' Kirby heard himself say. 'I've been insulted by the best in the business.' He flashed a wry smile. 'Pleased to meet you, Jade, even if you don't seem to think too high of me.'

She seemed slightly mollified by his easy manner, managing a half-smile before her father said, 'Everybody is edgy today.'

'Is that killer still about, Dad?' she asked, glancing both ways along the street.

'I haven't sighted him in a couple of hours, but I believe he has not left town . . . ' Craig's voice trailed off as he shook his head. 'Our mayor and sheriff snuffed out in a day . . . where do we go from here?'

'I said you folks should send for the marshal from Villanova,' Kirby put in. 'But your father didn't seem to go for that notion.'

The girl studied him soberly. She wore a dark-blue dress with a light-blue knitted shawl draped about slender shoulders. Up close, Kirby saw there was strength in her elfin face as well as beauty.

'They're saying that because all three men had guns in hand at the time of the shooting, then Fabian cannot be charged over the deaths of Hinch and Doolin. But I suspect you'd know that, Lee?'

'Still got me tabbed as one of Fabian's breed, huh?' he countered.

She studied him soberly and for once Lee Kirby felt less than confident. But then she surprised him when she said, 'I don't see the same cruelty in your face as I saw in that other man. But I'm afraid you still have the look of some kind of gunman to me.'

'You're honest,' he shrugged. 'Mind if I'm honest back?'

'Of course not.'

'You're scared stiff. So is your dad and every man-Jack in this town.'

'Surely that can't surprise you!' she exclaimed. 'He killed those men this morning and shows no sign of leaving. Who's to say he won't kill again?'

Kirby looked from one to the other narrowly as he asked, 'Wonder if Fabian might have had a special reason for picking this town?' He spread his hands. 'How come, you might ask? Well, I haven't been here long but I know already this is no ordinary town. It's odd, plenty odd.'

They demanded an explanation. He gave it readily.

'I know cow towns and this is more than a cow town. How come I'm so sure? Prosperity is how. Other towns, folks look like it's hard to make ends meet, but here I see blacksmiths wearing broadcloth and a liveryman in hand-tooled boots. Heck, I even see newspapermen packing their daughters off East to get educated.' He paused for effect. 'No sir, too much dinero about for this spot on the map to be anything like ordinary.'

Suddenly Craig appeared to lose interest as he mounted the steps. 'We'll have coffee at another time, Mr Kirby. I'm really played out. See you tomorrow, maybe?'

'Yeah, maybe.'

Suddenly he was alone. He shrugged as the door closed upon the couple, then turned away, feeling his pockets for a cigar.

They hadn't liked what he'd said, and he felt he'd touched a nerve. The fact that Macallister seemed uncommonly prosperous, and that its citizens were shy about it, encouraged him to believe that the rumour of hidden riches could be true.

He was nodding to himself as he entered Trail Street again, convinced now that this man's town would bear closer scrutiny.

He found himself alone on the tree-lined street, but they were still drinking at the Diamondback and Fat Libby's.

Kirby could feel the fear and tension

as he moved through the pools of light beneath the glass candle lamps. He didn't blame them for being jittery after three killings. It was plain that any man who'd kill so ruthlessly could easily do it again.

He paused opposite the hotel to stare both ways along Trail. He knew he was looking for any sign of that guntoter.

So — why had Fabian suddenly appeared in Macallister? Could it simply be coincidence that brought that gunslick to the same town which had aroused the interest of Kirby and his new henchmen of the owlhoot?

Or might there be more to it?

Was it possible that the brutal slaying of three citizens could be in some way connected with the secrets of Macallister which Kirby hoped to uncover?

There was no telling. Yet Kirby stepped warily and kept right hand close to gun handle as he crossed to his hotel and went inside.

But he saw no danger, nor was he meant to. He was halfway up the stairs before movement stirred in the maw of an alley alongside the City Billiard Parlour and a man emerged to stare after him thoughtfully.

For once, Fabian was without his slick cat smile. Like Kirby, the man of the gun was looking deeply thoughtful . . .

★   ★   ★

Uncertainty shadowed Jade Craig's face as she prepared for bed. Although a very pretty girl, and accustomed to the attentions of men, she found her meeting with Lee Kirby disturbing.

She'd been uncompromising towards the man, and felt that was justified. He did have the look of trouble about him, and she was certain he was skilled with that .45 which was worn with such familiarity.

Yet despite the tough impression he created, along with the fact that he appeared oddly curious about Macallister and its affairs, she already realized he'd made more of an impact upon her than any man she'd met in Colorado since her return from college to help out on her father's newspaper.

Getting into bed with moonlight spilling through her window, she suspected that for more than one reason she would not find it easy to sleep . . .

* * *

Moss O'Shea warmed his hands by wrapping them around a fresh mug of coffee and watched his sleeping henchmen snore the night away.

A calm white moon rode the eastern sky above Bracken Canyon. Moss O'Shea was forty-eight years of age and although he'd put in an eighteen-hour day, he'd still volunteered to stand night watch.

The outlaw leader wasn't motivated by generosity in this, he was simply too restless to sleep.

None of his hellions knew how much

he was relying upon success in Macallister. There'd been a long string of setbacks recently and Moss was feeling old and weary. He yearned for a big haul so he could go off to warm his 48-year-old bones in the Mexico sun and rejuvenate himself with old whiskey and young women.

He hoped events would prove his judgement sound in choosing Kirby to go to Macallister. He'd have gone himself only he'd likely have been shot or hanged if he dared show his well-publicized and big-nosed face in any town in Colorado at that moment.

He sighed gustily. The curse of notoriety!

He knew it would be doubly good in Old Mexico where nobody had even heard of Moss O'Shea or seen his portrait staring down from a thousand Wanted dodgers. Rich, free and anonymous. They were big goals for a man to set himself, based on nothing stronger than the drunken babble of that man from Macallister they'd encountered down in Helltown. But then, Moss had always been both a gambler and an optimist.

'This one'll pay off,' he told the whispering wind and a pale old moon. 'I just know it . . .

3

Only the Fastest

'Come and get it!' Kentucky Phil hollered. 'Afore she hits!'

Strolling by the diner on his way to the barber's for a shave the following morning, Kirby, who planned to eat later, was sufficiently intrigued to ask the obvious question, 'Before what hits, friend?'

Kentucky Phil eyed him pityingly. Out-of-towners sure enough were an ignorant breed, his expression said.

'Why . . . that, of course!' he stated, jabbing a fat finger southwards. 'The duster.'

Following the man's eyeline Kirby sighted the angry red cloud on the horizon beyond Buzzard Butte slowly spreading across the morning-blue sky.

'Headin' this way, you figure?'

'I don't figure, stranger, I know. And once we get wrapped up inside a genuine red duster at this time of the year, nobody feels like eatin' after windin' up with a gutful of sand. So what do you say? Eat now and starve later?'

'I reckon it'll pass us by to the east.'

'You claimin' you know more about the weather than me?'

'In a word — yeah.'

'You a wagerin' man?'

'I've been known to lay a bet. I've got five bucks to say you're wrong.'

'You're on,' Phil said, tugging bills from his pocket. He jerked a thumb over his shoulder. 'My cook'll hold the dinero. I'll get him to whip you up some breakfast chow while you're here.'

Kirby grinned as he followed the man inside. Mostly he felt bushy-tailed, mornings, and today was no exception. The hash house proprietor was a breezy sort, and he realized he was hungrier than he knew when the aroma of steak and frying bacon hit his nostrils.

The cook took the wagers then whipped up a fragrant dish of ham, eggs and chili while Kentucky Phil talked about the day's scheduled funerals in the same cheerful way he'd discussed the weather.

'Long time since we seen a trebler in Macallister, Lee. It'd go back to '76 when we had the cholera, I'd hazard. You be goin' along?'

'Why should I? I didn't know them.'

'Just had a feeling you seem powerful interested in our town, is all.'

Kirby swallowed bacon and washed it down with first-rate coffee. 'Who says I'm interested in your lousy town?'

'You been askin' plenty questions about us.'

Kirby speared another chunk of bacon, forked it into his jaws, chewed vigorously. These rubes were smarter than they looked, he mused.

'Mebbe I'm just naturally nosy,' he said non-committally. He looked around. He was Kentucky Phil's sole customer, yet even when largely empty the place maintained that same solid air of prosperity as every other business place he'd seen in town. 'Like, I'm kinda curious about how you folks here seem to thrive on practically nothing.'

'Just lucky I reckon. More java?'

'No, this'll hold me.' Kirby leaned back and extracted a fat cigar. 'So, tell me Phil, do you know a feller named Pracy?'

'Mace Pracy?'

'That's the party. So, you do know him, I take it?'

'Did. He was kicked outa town for molestin' a female a month back.' Kentucky Phil's eyes narrowed. 'Where'd you know him?'

'South,' was the vague reply. Kirby had not known of the molesting matter. Pracy had told him he'd quit Macallister because it was a boring hick town. Of course, Pracy had told them something else, which was the reason the gang had ridden two hundred hard miles to get there. Fast.

Kentucky Phil lost interest in conversation, excused himself and vanished somewhere in the rear. Paying his bill, Kirby went into the sunlight where towners in their Sunday best were on the streets, heading for either church or funeral parlour.

It was interesting, Kirby mused, to see a town putting on a brave face. He could see that every man, woman and child who passed by appeared jittery, even though their general manner was pale and grave. Macallister had grit, he decided. He knew towns that would panic with a buzzard like Fabian around.

And speaking of the devil . . .

The man in the brown rig and hat came along the walk with a quick, light-footed jauntiness. He was smiling in the sunshine and there was a hint of something obscene about the smile on the face of a man who'd just slain three men. His gun handles caught the light, jutting from their holsters, and Kirby, leaning against an upright now, was aware of the pale-blue eyes studying him closely as the gap between them narrowed.

He was not surprised when Fabian halted directly before him.

'You're Kirby?'

'Yeah. And you're Fabian.'

'Correct. What you doing here, Kirby?'

Kirby couldn't conceal his surprise. 'Ain't it a free country?'

'I asked a simple question.'

A faint warning bell buzzed inside Kirby's skull. He was not afraid of the man, but neither was he anxious to get into any sort of wrangle with him. There was no point in doing so.

He forced a smile and said, 'I'm just passing through, is all.'

'Why all the questions?'

'What questions would they be?'

'The ones you been asking about me all over town, is what — saddle bum!'

Kirby's eyes turned chill. There was always a limit to how much he would take from any man.

He moved down two steps to stand very close to the smaller man, letting him feel the full weight of his eyes. 'And now, unless you're about to ask what colour socks I'm wearing, I'll be moseying on.'

He waited, giving the other full opportunity to react. But Fabian just dropped his eyes until Kirby snapped his hat brim and walked off, heading for the barber's down the street. There was a store window opposite and he watched the gunman's reflection in the glass, alert for any sudden moves.

But Fabian didn't make any, seemingly content just to watch him until he entered the barber's shop. Only then did he continue on his way, swashbuckling down the walk in the sunshine as if he were Macallister's hero and not its villain.

The barber was gabby but Kirby remained silent during his shave. He had much on his mind. Having met Fabian face to face, he found it hard to believe that it was merely chance that had brought that man to Macallister, and was keeping him here.

There was something else . . . and he wondered if that 'something' might be silver. The kind they dug out of the ground. The sort of silver they got from that secret mine Mace Pracy had babbled about in Helltown.

★　★　★

'Good men one and all,' Parson Flynn proclaimed.

'Fine, upstanding Christian fathers, husbands and friends to a man, they were. *Vale*, our beloved brothers, and may the Almighty's wrath descent like a thunderbolt upon the evil one responsible for their being committed to the cold and uncaring clay here today.'

The parson drank more than was good for him, and his church was falling down round his ears through lack of care and maintenance. But whenever called upon to say a few good words he was a match for any man of the cloth in Colorado. There was scarce a dry eye at the cemetery by this and there would be even fewer by the time he was all through.

The parson thrust a bony finger into the reddening sky as a hundred mourners bowed their heads and stared at the yawning holes in the earth that had just received their dead.

'And so the words spoken through Jeremiah the prophet were fulfilled. A voice was heard in Rama, wailing in loud laments; it was Rachel weeping for her children, and refusing all consolation because they were no more.'

'Amen!' chorused the throng, and the sound drifted over the weeds and the canting headstones, across the green slopes of grass as the sun splashed roofs of town to reach dimly the brown-garbed figure seated on the hotel porch where he was coaxing a tune from a battered harmonica.

The sun was high in a sky that was pure sapphire blue to the north but a deep and menacing red to the south.

The breeze was fitful, running before the coming dust storm. It would gust briefly, then die away altogether, only to restart from another direction. It was an uneasy day of heat and wind which seemed strangely in keeping with the town's uncertain mood.

Fabian paused in his harmonica playing to glance towards the cemetery as the strains of the final hymn died away altogether and the mourners began to drift off.

As the first returning citizens reached Trail Street, they heard him playing 'Danny Boy,' a doleful tune in keeping with the solemnity of the occasion. But as more mourner's straggled into the main stem, he switched to the jumpy strains of 'Brass Kitty', which most recognized as a popular song in the whore houses.

There was any amount of muttering and glowering from the mourners as they trekked by the hotel, but the killer only appeared vastly amused as he tapped his toe and played on. Then finally Parson Flynn arrived flanked by several leading citizens, and he could not conceal his outrage.

'A foulness has descended upon our lands!' he thundered, striking a pose in the middle of the watching street. 'Oh that but a single one of us had the might and the sureness of arm to smite the thing that so offends every Christian eye this sad day!'

Mitch Craig nudged the preacher's elbow in a warning way and tried to move him along. But the reverend's ire was up. Instead of permitting himself to be led away to the saloon to top up on what he'd already put away that day, he shook himself free of his friends and approached the hotel on almost steady legs, shaking a pointed finger.

'Mammon may excuse your evil, stranger, but the Saviour above never shall. Shame on you for all your accursed black deeds! A curse upon your wretched name forever! May the wrathful flames of Hades devour your living flesh for the sadness you bring upon this town this day!'

The killer quit playing. He leaned forward with an expression of amused tolerance.

'Enjoy a quote or two, do we, Holy Joe?' he jeered. 'Well, how about this one? 'A fool's mouth is his destruction and his lips are the snare of the soul!''

'You mock us,' Flynn accused bitterly. 'It is not enough for your kind to kill and bereave, but you feel obliged to add mockery to the bitter brew. At times like this I wonder how the Lord can allow such good men to die and such unworthy ones to survive.'

Fabian nodded yet barely smiled now.

'Gabby, like all preachers,' he sneered. 'But now you're beginning to bother me, bible-basher.' He tapped his harmonica upon the heel of his hand. 'How about some marching music to lift the spirits?'

Flynn began to protest but Craig stepped forward and began dragging the man away. The man of the cloth struggled and Fabian looked on with mounting annoyance.

Jade Craig hurried across and put a hand on Flynn's arm.

'Please, Reverend,' she urged as the gunman looked on with a different expression taking command of his features. 'Don't say any more. There's nothing to be gained. Come away with us.'

'*Please, Reverend!*' Fabian mimicked. He shook his head as he rose and slipped the harmonica away. 'Oh, if I'd only had such a lovely caring lady to steer me right all those years ago, I mightn't have turned into the bad, terrible man I am today!'

Jade shot the gunman a cold glance but made no response. Instead, she tugged at the parson's arm, and he began to give ground, with some of the hectic heat fading from his face as he moved off with her.

'You're right of course, Jade dear . . . nothing else to be done now . . . '

'Wait!'

The killer's voice crackled with sudden incisive command. As the group paused, he came down the steps, his eyes fixed upon Jade Craig as he spoke. It was a hungry look, unnerving.

'Jade . . . now that surely is a jewel of a name. Come on back here, green-eyed Jade, and let me take a closer look. Who knows? Maybe you really are the angel I've been searching for all my life?'

'You don't want anything with my daughter,' Craig said. 'Come along, Jade, Reverend.'

'So speaks the editor!' Fabian mocked. 'You forget these ain't just words you're dealing with here, scrawler, but flesh and blood.' He almost laughed. 'Your blood and her flesh? Who knows?' He crooked a finger. 'Come here, Jade.'

She lifted her chin, slender and small in her funereal black. 'You might frighten some people on this town, gunman, but not me.'

'You should be afraid.'

'What will you do if I defy you? Murder me as you did those three good men yesterday?'

'That's a thought.'

'And would you call that self-defence as well?' she defied him. 'Shooting down an unarmed woman?'

'What I'd call it, would be a terrible waste. Now, quit acting the fishwife and get back here, Jade baby. I want to talk with you, and what Fabian wants, he gets, in case you don't know it.'

'Varlet!' the parson cried, steamed up once again. 'Is there no limit to your perfidy?' With that he slipped a protective arm around Jade's shoulders and began leading her away. 'You'd be better occupied pleading with your Maker for forgiveness, rather than adding to your sins by terrorizing an innocent — '

The parson's voice was engulfed by the shuddering thunder of a gunblast, and his black hat spun into the air and then fell away with a small, smoking hole through the crown.

Every eye was focused upon the .45 in Fabian's fist.

'Last chance,' he warned a white-faced Jade Craig as the reverberations slowly faded. 'Walk back here, Miss High-and-mighty, or you won't walk anywhere again.'

Would he carry out his threat? None could tell.

Maybe there was indeed no limit to what a coldblooded killer was capable of. Maybe Hinch, Walters and Doolin had just been a start. Maybe the yellow-haired butcher planned on going on killing until there was nobody left. Or until somebody killed him.

Until somebody killed him.

The thought seared like a white-hot branding iron across Lee Kirby's brain as he stepped from the cool dark doorway of the livery stables opposite. He'd seen it all, sensed when it threatened to turn ugly, then seen it do so. He walked neither quickly nor slowly towards the hotel with his heels sucking in the dust. His right hand was wrapped around his gun and the hammer was on full cock.

As he came in down Fabian's flank, the gunman was one of the last to become aware of him. Surprise jumped into his eyes as he span, only to be instantly replaced by something far more deep and lethal.

'Saddle bum!'

'Put up that gun!' Kirby ordered. 'Put it up, then get your horse and get to hell and gone from this town, gunboy. You've just used up the last of your welcome.'

'*Gunboy?*'

The word seemed to scald Fabian's tongue. Yet he was grinning again as he rammed his Colt back into leather and backed up a pace with both hands suspended over loaded holsters.

'Is this what it looks like, saddle bum? A real, honest-to-God challenge? Judas Priest! It's so long since any son-of-a-bitch idiot was fool enough to call me out fair-and-square this way that I've near to forgotten what the thrill was like!'

'No!' Jade cried as Kirby came to a halt a bare fifty feet distant from the smirking gunshark. 'Lee, don't. He'll kill you!'

'My daughter's right, man,' Craig shouted. 'This man is a professional killer. Don't sacrifice yourself!'

But Kirby wasn't listening. He couldn't afford to. Everything in him was concentrated upon Fabian. He sensed how fast this man was — and knew he daren't give him a whisper of an advantage.

'Either shuck those dude guns or use them, Fabian!' he challenged.

He drew some comfort from catching the faintest glimpse of uncertainty in the other's baleful stare. Fabian was reacting to his flinty self-assurance, he sensed, maybe figuring that anybody that cock-sure likely *must* be good?

Yet even if impressed against his will, the killer wasn't daunted. Not Fabian, the two-gun killer who reminded old greybeard Petrie of Billy the Kid. This was Fabian's forte — the familiar drama of dust, sun and imminent bloodshed. He was at his best. He was ready to play out the leader's role and wear the victor's laurel wreath once again.

He drew.

Kirby had never faced a man as fast. His gun-speed didn't seem real. And yet it was.

Kirby proved almost as swift — and he also had a trick taught to him by an old gun champion that had more than once saved his life. As he came clear, he went down on one knee. Top guns like Fabian always shot for the head, for a man with a bullet in his brain can never pull a trigger.

Lead hissed harmlessly over the crown of Kirby's hat as he went low, and he heard Jade Craig scream and saw Fabian's eyes snap wide when he realized his shot had missed.

Then Kirby's own piece thundered. One shot. The bullet smacked between the killer's eyes with an impact that jolted the fine brown hat from his head. Instantly, the killer's bones seemed to turn to jelly and he fell in the dust with his smoking gun still locked in his fist and the sky red above him — but he was unaware of any of it.

Kirby didn't realize he'd become an instant hero even before he'd risen slowly to his feet.

4

Silver Town

Kirby sat by the courthouse window idly watching wind-blown sand peppering the glass.

He was down five dollars, having bet that the day would be fine and sunny. Mostly he guessed right where the weather was concerned, but not today. It was mid-afternoon and Macallister was in the grip of a howling norther that had cleared the streets and was now whipping the cottonwoods and peppercorns all along the main stem into a frenzy.

So it was a lousy day and he was losing money! Yet Kirby was still grinning because today found him whole and unscathed and still alive to taste sand in his coffee. It could blow for a week straight and he wouldn't grouch about it.

There were six others in the jail office with him, Mitch Craig and the five citizens who constituted what remained of the Macallister Town Council.

He'd thought at first that the councillors had showed up to vote their official thanks to him for ridding them of Fabian the shootist, and he'd already been so thanked. Then the six had then withdrawn to a corner for several minutes to confer, and he speculated they might be discussing some kind of reward for him for what the parson himself had described as his 'Saving our town'.

He wanted no reward. He'd killed Fabian simply because he'd had to be killed, and no other reason. Besides, if things went according to plan, this town was destined to suffer at his hands before he was through.

He could do without the irony of honest folks rewarding a man who meant to rob them blind.

The yammering wind beat constantly

against the jailhouse walls and pried into every crevice. Kirby could even taste the dust as he drew upon his crooked black Mexican cigar. Faintly through the reddish haze he could see the lights of the funeral parlour glowing. The undertaker was at work. He'd been busier this week than at any time since the cholera epidemic.

Although Kirby showed no outward sign of it, the killing had hit him hard. He'd been born with a natural skill for a Colt .45, but drew no special pleasure from using one.

He continued to puzzle upon the gunman's presence in Macallister, which had been aggravated by the man carrying on like some fast-gun adolescent from the piney woods. It was rare that top-liners of that calibre went about killing just for the thrill of it. Most always there was money attached to their activities yet there was nothing to suggest that Fabian might have been hiring his gun out to anybody.

A faint frown etched his brow. Could it be that Fabian had also caught a whiff of the secret silver mine?

But again, there seemed to be nothing to support that notion either.

Fabian had come and gone in a blaze of gunfire, and that might well be the end to it. Peculiar, maybe, but no great mystery. Kirby wasn't about to lose any sleep over it. In the murderous world of the fast-gun kings, the winners always smiled while the losers fed the worms.

Smoke trickled from the gunfighter's lips as he turned his head. The good men of the council were approaching, led by Craig. They wore the fatuous expressions of men about to pop a big surprise. Kirby was fast getting bored with the whole deal. His throat had felt dry as a rusted iron pipe ever since the gun battle. He wanted some of that fine blended whiskey they served at the Diamondback, and if these men wanted to treat him he would be happy to accept that as a reward.

But they didn't.

Instead, they offered him the fully-paid post of town sheriff.

Kirby eyed them coldly. 'You can only be joking. But I don't have any sense of humour. Nobody offers jobs like that to any saddle stiff who comes wandering in through the tall trees. Nobody!'

'We figure you're one hell of a lot more than any saddle stiff, Lee,' Craig smiled. 'If we didn't feel that way, we wouldn't be makin' this here offer.'

'You're loco!' Lee snapped. 'You know nothing about me except I can handle a gun.'

'Which is likely the most important qualification of all hereabouts, man,' banker Stewart Swan put in. 'You see, this whole Fabian affair has driven home to us just how vulnerable Macallister really is, stuck away here on its lonesome in the middle of no place. Coe Walters was a fine peace officer yet when the chips were down he was hopelessly outclassed. But for your arrival, Macallister might well have been completely taken over by that murderous gunman. And who's to say another Fabian might not ride in tomorrow? But if we have a man of your calibre wearing the badge then there would be nothing to fear.'

'You still don't know enough about me,' Kirby reasoned.

This brought another smile from Craig.

'You risked your life because my daughter was in peril, Lee. The Fabian breed never does things like that. That action in itself told us you're a man of integrity, courage and honour. In short — exactly the breed of man we need to replace Coe Walters. So, what do you say?'

'I say you're loco.'

The councillors showed disappointment as Kirby quit his window spot and began moving restlessly about the room. His reaction to their offer was unexpected. But suddenly grey-bearded Petrie brightened as though enlivened by a fresh thought.

'Damnation, boys, can't you see it? We're settin' the cart before the horse offerin' the man a dangerous job of work with no mention of money!'

'Of course, you're right, Petrie,' Craig said eagerly. He nodded briskly to Kirby. 'One hundred dollars per month, Lee, plus all fine fees and free horse stabling. Now what do you say?'

Kirby made a curt dismissive gesture that looked far more emphatic than it really was. For he was immediately reminded that he'd been searching for something really worthwhile to do with his life for years now — and here it was being offered at long last. Even so, he'd never envisioned himself as a peace officer, was surprised that the prospect should appeal to him so strongly . . .

You're still a borderline outlaw and guntoter, the voice of hard cold conscience reminded him.

'No dice,' he growled, sounding like he meant it.

The councillors traded looks before Craig drew them into a huddle in the corner. He watched them cynically. Why were they so keen to sign him on, when any normal town would obviously go hire themselves a federal marshal and not just some stranger who happened to be handy with a gun?

Then a suspicion with even more impact to it hit home. Were they this eager to hire him because they didn't want outsiders — or nosy professional lawkeepers — knowing their secret?

He was stubbing his cigar butt out when Craig crossed to him and invited him to accompany him to the offices of the Macallister National Bank across the street. There was something there — or so the newsman insisted — that might well convince him to change his mind.

Kirby dickered with the notion of again saying no. He was no longer curious about what they might have to show him. But if he accepted, he'd feel obligated to pass the information on to his henchmen waiting at the canyon. He was no longer anything like certain he wanted to go on with his first owlhoot job now.

The councillors proved persuasive and Kirby's curiosity finally got the better of him.

'All right, damnit,' he said tersely, grabbing up his hat. 'But whatever it is, it ain't going to change my mind.'

'Don't be too sure, Lee,' Craig grinned as he led the way into the surging fog of dust.

* * *

It was very quiet in the bank vault with bright lamplight glinting silently from the silver ingots. The silver was stacked in neat piles on steel shelves, each imprinted with the name of Macallister National and identified by its own secret number. At a quick glance Kirby reckoned there were about twenty of the pieces stacked in the biggest and sturdiest-looking vault he'd ever seen outside cities like Denver or Kansas City.

'Well, Lee,' Craig said. 'What do you make of all this?'

Kirby licked dry lips before responding. There was enough silver here to set up the outlaw pack in luxury in Old Mexico with plenty to spare, he realized. He'd never seen so much dinero in one place before. It was a vivid reminder of what could drive a man to seek the outlaw life.

'What I'd say first,' he said with forced casualness, 'is that there has to be a sizeable silver mine hereabouts that I haven't heard about.'

'Your assumption is correct,' the newsman affirmed. 'So now do you see why we want someone like you to pin on the badge?'

'Let me get this straight,' Kirby said. 'You're telling me that nobody outside this town knows about this here mine?'

The councillors grinned proudly.

'The Crow Hill Mine is special, Lee. Whenever silver was first discovered here by Tom Petrie about a year ago we all sat down and discussed it, then came

73

to the conclusion we could do one of two things. We could tell the world and have our town crawling with fortune hunters from all over within a week — or we could all make it Macallister's secret.'

'We finally elected to keep it to ourselves,' Petrie chimed in. 'You see, son, I'm too old for riches now, but I love this here town and its folks. So I offered them all an equal share in the mine — providin' they swore to keep it secret from outsiders.'

'Which they did,' the banker stated proudly. 'You wouldn't believe so many men, women and kids could keep a thing like that to themselves for any length of time, but they did it. It's over twelve months now since Tom made his strike — and not a whisper of our big secret has seeped out in all that time.'

The man was almost right, Kirby mused. He could well have been one hundred per cent correct but for a character named Mace Pracy who'd been kicked out of town for poor behaviour — then shot off his mouth in a border jail.

'We're ready to offer you a share in the mine if you take on the job, Lee,' Craig insisted. 'We realize we're taking a risk, but it's a calculated one taken in the hope of you changing your mind. We're all just plain folks in Macallister. We don't know how to counter a man like Fabian. If someone got wind of our secret and set out to plunder us we'd be next door to helpless without someone of your calibre back us up.'

'You'll get the same cut as every other man does,' Petrie assured.

'A job and security for life, Kirby,' the newsman added persuasively. 'I don't reckon any man could want better than that.'

Suddenly Kirby wanted to be out of this strongroom with its glittering riches. He was confused and didn't care for that feeling. He needed to get outside where the wind was blowing clean in order to get his thoughts straightened out.

Which was exactly what he did.

The wind blew straight and hard and red dust stung his eyes as the councillors finally beat their way around the corner to sight his silhouette standing tall and lean against the whirling backdrop of the storm.

Kirby was barely aware of them. He was reflecting upon Moss O'Shea and what he might do if he got word his ex-partner Lee Kirby had ditched him to become Town Sheriff of Macallister.

He'd hoped the open air might clear his thinking, and it had. There could be no swapping horses in mid-stream!

'I'm not the man you want,' he tried to explain. 'Sorry.' And without another word, he strode off to be lost quickly in the surging storm.

It was six sober councillors who sought the refuge of Kentucky Phil's a short time later. They dropped into chairs and tugged off their hats while Phil got busy drawing coffee from his big nickel urn by the stove. As there were few secrets between one citizen and another, the hash house proprietor wasn't too long discovering the reason behind their disappointment.

'Too bad, boys,' he sighed solicitously. 'I reckon there's no doubt he was the man we wanted.'

'He didn't even nibble at the bait of a cut in the profits.' Stewart Swan sounded puzzled.

'If you ask me, he wasn't all that surprised to hear about the mine,' the newsman said thoughtfully.

This remark caused Kentucky Phil to glance up sharply.

'Not surprised . . . ?' he muttered. 'Say . . . that reminds me of somethin' Lee said while he was in here talkin' about the weather.' He paused, glancing from face to face. 'He mentioned Pracy.'

'Pracy?' Craig's manner was sharp. 'What did he say about him?'

'Just that he'd struck him some place else.'

Craig slowly lowered his coffee mug. 'I wonder . . . '

'What, Mitch?' Petrie pressed.

'Pracy was a mighty bitter man when we threw him out following that ugly business with the woman from Fat Libby's,' he said. 'I'm just wonderin' if he might have spilled our secret as a way of strikin' back at us?'

'You mean Lee might have heard about the mine beforehand?' Swan queried.

'I'm only guessing, Stew. But it does give a man food for thought, don't it?'

Heads nodded slowly but emphatically. All agreed it certainly was food for thought. And as the minutes slipped by, one thought led to another and some men were beginning to wonder if this town's period of peace and prosperity might suddenly be at an end.

Mitch Craig was the man who eventually put their thoughts into words.

If it was true that the banished Mace Pracy had shot his mouth, then not only Lee but also Fabian and maybe half the rogues and outlaws of the county could know the secret of Macallister.

★ ★ ★

Lee Kirby's six-gun hammer clicked back to full cock as the shadowy figure ghosted towards him along the crest of the brush-choked ridge above the canyon hideaway.

'Stand fast!' he barked abruptly.

'Kirby?' came the familiar voice of Joe Rolfe. The grey-haired outlaw hove closer and squinted over the bandana drawn up over nose and mouth. 'Figgered it was you,' he said at last in muffled voice. He gestured back at the dim outline of the canting boulder. 'Let's get back under cover quick, son. This here wind's blowin' hard enough to make a man forget his religion.'

Kirby was relieved to take shelter behind the giant boulder, for the duster had been handing him a hammering every mile between Macallister and Bracken Canyon.

'How'd you make out, Kirby? We been gettin' a mite edgy, waitin'.'

'Pay dirt,' Kirby grunted. 'Seems Pracy was telling the truth all along. They got a mine and a bank vault stuffed with pure silver.'

Rolfe chuckled. He was a tough, square-bodied man of around forty who was the only member of the gang Kirby liked. Rolfe seemed less greedy and violent than the others, and Kirby reckoned he might be tolerably smarter also. With the exception of O'Shea, of course.

'Moss is goin' to be tickled, Kirby. What's the story?'

Kirby supplied a full account and Rolfe's eyes stretched to full limit.

'You gunned Fabian and they offered you the job of sheriff? Glory be, Kirby, and here he was out here picturin' you sittin' around in some saloon pinchin' bottoms.'

'I can tell you he was fast.'

'How fast?'

'No describin' it,' Kirby said with a

humourless smile. 'But I knew more tricks.'

Rolfe studied the man with new respect. 'Y'know, I've heard of that Fabian. He used to be big-time.'

'Yeah. And that's what puzzles me, Joe. What was a big gun like him doin' in Macallister? I'm wonderin' if we're the *only* ones Pracy talked to.'

'Well, the sound of hard cash travels a long ways, Kirby. But, hell, this sure is great news any ways you look at it, son. Let's you and me get our gritty carcasses out of this damned storm and go tell Moss. He's gettin' mighty anxious.'

Leading his horse and tugging his kerchief up over his nose again, Kirby started off with Rolfe at his side toting his rifle. It was less than a hundred yards from the ridge to the battered wolvers' cabin which the band had claimed, yet even in that short distance the dust finally blew itself out in a single great boisterous gust of sound and was gone, howling away into the north leaving an eerie silence and a few chinks of blue sky in its noisy wake.

'It's an omen!' Moss O'Shea declared, his gesture inviting everybody to take a look at the big slice of blue sky some time later after Kirby had lodged his full report. 'Looks like clear skies for this lucky old bunch from here on in.'

The man clapped Kirby on the back as they moved onto the porch to gaze at a world hazed over with a fine film of dust.

'Had a feelin' about you the first day I clapped eyes on you, son, sure enough. Said then you shaped up as the genuine article. Didn't I say that to you boys?'

Rolfe, Tanner, Flint and Hannigan all nodded. Sure enough, the boss man had predicted big things for new man Kirby, and who could contest that he'd been anything but right. The O'Shea bunch was staring at its biggest success ever, and not one of the bunch could stop from grinning right now.

Feeling curiously flat Kirby just grunted and put a light to a fresh cigar. He puffed the weed into life as he paced around, watching the clear footprints he left in the dust. Kirby finally halted and turned to O'Shea.

'It's a hick town but they've got a solid bank and one hell of a vault. They might have lost their sheriff, but they are sure as hell still on the alert. Even though we know about the silver, gettin' it won't be any cinch. We'll need a smart plan.'

'Well, I've figured out the first and most important part of it, son,' O'Shea grinned, slapping him on the back yet again.

'What part's that?'

'Why, the part where you hustle back to town to tell 'em you'd surely admire to take on that job they so kindly offered, of course. This is shapin' up as the first time I ever cracked any town with the help of the *law*!'

5

This Man's Star

The easing of the dust storm came as a welcome relief to the travellers aboard the north-bound stage. The driver and gun guard had wanted to sit out the duster back in Dalton, but the paying passengers had insisted they push on. Normally, the crew would have overridden the passengers, but not this time. Although Solway Booth and his three companions wore suits, bowler hats and elastic-sided boots, they didn't really look or act like businessmen.

The stage crew noted that each man packed at least one weapon, and though Booth was a smooth-spoken and immaculately polite gentleman, there was more than a hint of menace in the eyes behind the pince-nez.

So the crew had decided that it

would prove more comfortable to journey on through a dust storm than become locked in a wrangle with a tough bunch like this. As a result the lifting of the storm found them within a couple of hours' travel of Macallister, whereas had they stopped at Dalton they would likely still be facing half a day's travel.

'Roll down the windows,' Booth ordered as the coach and six approached the first of many Cross Creek crossings. His order was promptly obeyed and he sat staring at the eerie pink-dust landscape, his hands folded neatly in his lap, smooth features expressionless.

'Do you reckon this here looks anythin' like silver country, boss?' asked Wannamaker, a slab of a man with ox shoulders straining against the seams of a too-tight jacket.

'Possibly, possibly,' Solway Booth replied, modulated voice matching his cultivated appearance. A man of middling size and indeterminate age, he was always immaculately attired whereas his companion merely put on anything that fitted. With pince-nez, gold watch chain, neatly knotted silk tie and stylish hat, Booth might have passed as a successful banker, cattle dealer, railroad tycoon or politician.

The man looked nothing like he really was, namely a deadly outlaw as ruthless and coldblooded as any swaggering, gun-packing hell-raiser who walked the West.

He looked nothing like what he really was, an outlaw of the first dimension and as dangerous as any Jack Vane or Kid Billy you might be unlucky enough to meet.

Wannamaker, Jackson and Ketch, on the other hand, looked pretty much what they really were. Wannamaker's giant size, Jackson's scarred visage and Ketch's stealthy, cat-like presence marked them all down as rough characters, smart business suits notwithstanding.

Yet Booth felt confident that Macallister would accept them as dealers in livestock and lumber, which was their cover. They would be accepted mainly because Solway Booth would convince the hicks that his companions were strictly legitimate simply because they travelled with him.

Whenever he really put his mind to it, Booth could all but convince a gullible person that up was down.

The horses strained up a steep rise with the crew jolting up on the box. The gun guard clutched his shotgun while the driver worked the long leather ribbons expertly until a giant split opened up in the red sky and the afternoon sun sought to struggle through.

'Only about ten miles now,' came the response. 'We'll be stoppin' off to water the hosses a couple of miles ahead, then straight on to town.'

Booth grunted and leaned back. The others were lighting up cigars but Booth did not indulge. His only real vices were young women and greed. He lusted endlessly after young women, but would kill in cold blood for silver or gold. And visions of wealth beyond all limits brought a smile to his mouth as the coach lurched and staggered down through the ridges towards the way station at Cosgrove's Crossing.

'Wonder if they got any liquor at the stop-off?' Jackson speculated. 'I'm drier than a Death Valley powder-house the day after a duster, b'God!'

'No booze,' Booth growled. 'Not for anybody until we get the lie of the land in Macallister.'

Jackson looked distraught.

'Boss, you know what I'm like if I don't get a taste of somethin'. I get fidgety. Ornery even.'

'You won't be getting ornery in Macallister,' he was warned. 'You'll be just the same as the rest of us, Jackson. Upright, helpful, and eager to please. Compre?'

Jackson sighed and nodded. This was a new kind of operation for him. His technique when he wanted something belonging to somebody else was to haul a gun and take it. This style had landed him in deep trouble many a time, but Booth was teaching him how to be a crook and still stay out of jail. Booth planned to plunder Macallister without a shot being fired. Or, more correctly, without another shot being fired.

The coded wire Booth had received from Fabian down south had told him that several very effective shots had already been fired early in the Macallister campaign.

Booth smiled again. Were all his men as reliable as Fabian then success was guaranteed. The smile faded quickly. But, of course, Fabian had his short-comings, as Booth was well aware. Sometimes he killed far too readily. He was like a performing tiger in a circus, which underneath, would always be a jungle animal no matter how well disciplined.

A battered old way station loomed ahead and the driver swung the dusty team into the littered yard and sawed to a halt. Stiffly, protestingly, passengers and crew climbed down while a man appeared carrying water buckets for the horses.

Booth flicked dust from his coat and walked about to stretch his legs, twirling the silver-topped cane. A sour-faced agent called Jack brought out coffee in mugs on a tray, which Booth declined. He had his standards, particularly where his stomach was concerned.

Solway Booth was forced to take delicate care of his stomach.

'Nice place you got here,' Ketch offered the agent, intent on practising his friendly businessman role.

'It stinks,' replied the man.

'You sure said it,' Wannamaker rapped without thinking. Then, catching a warning flash of pincenez, he smiled and said, 'Er . . . no, I agree it's a right, fine-lookin' spot you got here. You get into Macallister often, partner?'

'Never!' The agent was plainly a man in whose veins the *joie de vivre* had ceased to throb — if it ever had done.

'Hate towns and towners. You fellers towners?'

'Country folk,' Ketch declared. 'We're in cattle and lumber.'

The agent wasn't impressed. 'Splinters and cowpats. Who needs 'em?'

'Don't pay Jack no never-mind, folks,' the paunchy guard grinned. 'He's been down on the world ever since his missus run off to be a saloon dancer back in the fifties. Ain't that so, Jack?'

'Could be,' the mournful man muttered. His brown creased. 'But, funny thing though, I was always of the opinion Macallister shaped up as a better town than most until just the day afore yesterday . . . '

'Why, what happened then?' the driver prompted.

'Mean you ain't heard? Hell, three fellers got mowed down so they did, and that included the mayor and the sheriff!'

'The hell you say!' breathed the gun guard. 'Coe Walters was a friend of mine. Who in hell shot 'em?'

Booth drifted closer to listen as the agent cleared his throat.

'Some out-of-town gunslick named Fable, or somethin' like. Braced the mayor and the water-carter in the Diamondback. Chopped 'em both down then blasted Sheriff Walters when he come a-runnin'. Three funerals in the one day! Sure glad I got the sense to stay clear of towns, yessir.'

'What happened to the bastard what shot 'em?' the guard demanded angrily. 'Did they get him?'

Booth leaned closer to hear, even though certain he already knew the answer. But he was mistaken.

'Yup,' Jack replied, spitting again.

'*What*' Booth said sharply. 'What do you mean?'

'I mean he's dead,' Jack said emphatically. 'Finished. Croaked. In the sod.'

Booth was incredulous. 'You must be mistaken,' he blurted out.

'Well, there be four new graves in Macallister,' the agent stated lugubriously. 'The three I mentioned and their killer. That's sin-ridden towns for you.'

'What happened to Fabian?' Wanna-maker demanded. The two had ridden together in Mexico before joining up with Solway Booth.

'Gunned down,' Jack supplied lugu-briously, plainly enjoying the effect his news was having. 'Outdrawed and shot stone dead by some stranger name of Kirby.' He paused to look from one face to the other. 'Say . . . you gents look kind of shook. You know any of them folks?'

'Know them?' Booth's cultured voice was thick. He paused and cleared his throat. 'Er, no, of course not. We're strangers here. It's just . . . well, just such an ugly story, is all.'

'That about the only sort of story that ever comes out of them dot-rotted towns, mister,' Jack commented pre-dictably. 'Sure you don't want that mug of coffee. You look like you could use one.'

Booth shook his head. His sensitive stomach was giving him enough hell already without adding to it. In truth, Solway Booth felt just like a man who'd been kicked in the belly by a mean horse. Fabian getting himself killed was the one thing he'd not planned on when mapping out his scheme to plunder Macallister of its secret treasure.

For, like just about everybody who knew Fabian, Booth had regarded that killer as invincible . . .

* * *

In the late afternoon, Mitch Craig was setting type at the *Courier* office while his daughter put the finishing touches to her article on the story which would carry the banner heardline:

MORE VIOLENCE IN MACALLISTER!

'I suppose a newspaper should never look a gift horse in the mouth, Dad,' the girl sighed glumly. 'At least these days we don't have to go hunting for news . . . '

'No news is bad news, Jade,' Craig said glumly. 'But four men dead in just two days . . . it's still hard to believe . . . '

'I'm not satisfied with this story,' Jade remarked after a silence. 'It tells everything except the most important part. Why? Why did Fabian come to Macallister and kill three men for no reason? And where did Lee bob up from? What value is a story without answers to the questions people are asking?'

'We're reporters, not lawmen, Jade,' Craig reminded, staring out the window. 'We don't have the answers and maybe never will . . . '

Jade studied her father carefully. She knew him better than anyone — and knew when he had something on his mind.

She rose from her desk and crossed to him, dark skirt and white blouse emphasising the trimness of her figure.

'What is it, Dad? It's something about Lee Kirby, isn't it? Don't you feel I have the right to know what happened between him and you yesterday?'

'We offered him the sheriff's post and he turned us down.'

'Is that all?'

'Not quite all. Later, I heard from Kentucky Phil that Kirby had asked him about Mace Pracy.'

'I don't understand. Why should that bother you?'

'Because Pracy was thrown out of Macallister. He was the first man to leave town since we struck silver. It occurred to me that Pracy might have, well . . . talked.'

Understanding dawned in Jade's face.

'Talked to Kirby, you mean?'

'Could have done.'

'Then you're suggesting it's the silver that brought him here?'

'It's a possibility,' Craig said with a shrug. 'Who knows? Perhaps the same thing drew Fabian, too? We don't know how many might have heard of the mine before Pracy got himself killed down south.'

'Surely you can't believe Kirby is a crook?'

'I wouldn't go that far, Jade. But I am worried. If the secret of the mine is out, then we must take steps to protect ourselves before it's too late.'

'Perhaps you're jumping to conclusions, Dad. After all, Kirby didn't say he knew about the silver, did he?'

'No.'

'Then I wouldn't worry about it too much. In any case, even if he did know, I don't think it would pose much risk.'

'Any outsider having that knowledge poses a risk, Jade. And now Kirby knows for certain. I'm beginning to wonder if it was wise telling him after all . . . '

'You were simply trying to persuade him to take the sheriff's post, Dad. You had to bait the hook.'

'Know something, Jade?'

'What?'

'Every time I mention Lee Kirby, you stand up for him. Don't you think that's . . . curious?'

She looked away quickly, feigning interest in something outside.

'Why should that seem curious?'

'I can't recall you defending any other young man so staunchly. And the good Lord knows there have been any number of that particular variety hanging about ever since you came back from college.'

'Surely you're not implying that I might be interested in this . . . drifter?'

'Are you?'

'Of course not,' she said quickly. Much too quickly. She realized immediately she'd given something away she wished to keep to herself. Too late. Cutting a sideways glance at her father, she could see he had not missed her slip — for she had indeed cultivated a deep interest in the tall stranger with the deep eyes who'd killed in her defence.

Jade had been bitterly disappointed to learn that Kirby had quit town, and still nourished the hope that he would drift back into Macallister in the same casual way he'd left. But that slender hope was already fading fast . . .

She suddenly found herself staring out across the street as a rider rounded the bakery corner and headed directly towards the office.

'Dad!' she cried, immediately beginning to fuss with her hair and adjust her blouse. 'It's him. Lee!'

And Kirby it was. Riding directly to the hitch-rail, he swung down easily, tied his horse, then entered the office.

He removed his hat as he approached the wooden railing which divided the editorial section from the office area.

Both father and daughter welcomed him in a subdued manner, neither wishing to reveal just how pleased they were to see him again. Kirby, looking lean and bronzed in a freshly-laundered red shirt and moleskin pants, tipped his hat to Jade, nodded to Craig.

'Nice day, folks. After the dust, I mean.'

'A real fine day,' Craig said. 'What can I do for you, Kirby?'

'Just wondering if your job is still open?'

'The sheriff's posting? But I thought you weren't interested?'

'You kind of took me by surprise yesterday. I never pictured myself as a badgetoter, but thinking it over I figured maybe it was something worth trying.'

'Well . . . I'd have to consult the council,' Craig said. 'I'm only acting mayor.'

Lee eyed him sharply. 'You don't seem as keen as before, Mitch.'

'Well, to be honest, I didn't know you'd met Mace Pracy before,' Craig admitted.

'Pracy?' Lee appeared puzzled. 'Who's he?' Then he snapped his fingers. 'Ah, yes, now I recall. Say . . . what's all this about anyway?'

Craig glanced at his daughter and she was looking directly at him. He shook his head. 'Er, nothing important I guess, Lee.' He scrubbed the ink from his fingers with a swab of cotton waste then went to the rack for hat and coat. 'We're ahead with the work, Jade, so I'll go have a word with the councillors. Take half an hour off, yourself. Lee might even treat you to a cup of coffee?'

He was smiling as he made for the door.

'I'll put it to the men again, Kirby, and somehow I've a hunch they might still be interested in seeing you wear the badge . . . now.'

'And I'm completely sure of it,' Jade said, as she pinned on her bonnet. Her cheeks were pink and she couldn't keep from smiling. 'I'm so pleased you came back, Lee.'

'That makes two of us, Jade,' proffering his arm as they went out. 'Kentucky Phil's?'

'What's the alternative?'

'Afraid there ain't one, ma'am.'

'Then Kentucky Phil's sounds just fine.'

The following hour seemed to pass with astonishing speed for Jade Craig. She was half an hour late returning to her office, but didn't care simply because she'd so enjoyed the time spent in Lee's company . . .

He glanced at her — and caught her studying him. She blushed and he smiled. 'I'm sorry if I was staring.'

'Look all you care to . . . providing you don't mind me looking back.'

She turned and pretended to be occupied with her papers. She heard the soft chime of his spurs as he shifted his weight.

'You're one real pretty lady, Jade. But I guess you've been told that before?'

'Thank you. Now I really must get this piece finished before — '

'I've known lots of pretty women, but they weren't ladies.'

She turned to face him. He looked very serious, almost awkward.

'I'll take that as a compliment, Lee,' she replied warmly. 'Would you care to take a seat and wait for Dad?'

He accepted. He didn't have to wait long before Craig returned with banker Stewart Swan and Tom Petrie. Petrie had brought along a bible and a badge; the decision had been reached.

Kirby was sworn in as sheriff of Macallister and Craig took the oath as mayor. Jade decided the proceedings called for a celebration and left the article for her father to complete while she hurried home to prepare a celebration spread.

On the way, she saw the northbound stage swing in and pull up at the Trail Street depot. At another time she might have been curious about the four men who stepped down in sober suits, but she barely spared them a glance as she hurried on.

The senior of the four newcomers watched the girl walk out of sight, his pince-nez glinting and something dark and hungry coming alive in his eyes.

★ ★ ★

'You're drunk, mister,' Macallister's new sheriff stated.

'Thash a dirty lie,' Rumpot Jake objected, then promptly lost his balance and fell, knocking himself out cold as an Aspen moonrise.

Kirby grinned as he turned to Jake's drinking partners at Fat Libby's long bar.

'Tote him home and see he stays there,' he ordered.

'Right away, Sheriff.'

Sheriff.

It would take some time, getting used to that handle, Kirby reflected, but he was prepared to work on it. He'd held down many a job in his day but none had ever given him a boost like this one. And yet he'd only had it for just a few short hours.

He reckoned he could also get accustomed to the star on his chest — given time.

Drinkers, percentage girls and the cross-eyed piano player watched him warily as he moved about the tables checking on the gambling layouts. They'd seen his gun battle with Fabian, which guaranteed these small fish at least would treat him with respect.

Word had gone out that Sheriff Kirby had been informed of Macallister's secret and, as always, the man in the street was prepared to stand by the council's judgement in such an important matter . . .

'Buy you a shot, Sheriff honey?' a feminine voice murmured, and Kirby turned to see the same faded blonde who'd accosted him his first night in town.

'Later maybe. Thanks, anyway.'

'You're welcome, handsome. Say, you've sure came a long way fast in this town, ain't you?'

'If you say so.'

'I surely do. Funny thing, I had you figured for lots of things when you showed, but a lawman wasn't one of them.'

'This is my first badge job,'

'Proud of it, ain't you?'

He just nodded and moved on. The irony was that he genuinely was proud of the star he wore, even if the whole thing was just a sham and a mockery.

'Evening, Sheriff.'

Turning towards the voice he saw three of the four newcomers who'd arrived upon the afternoon stage. He'd been told they were dealers in cattle and timber, and they decidedly looked the part in their suits and hard-hitter hats.

It was the senior man who'd spoken. He tipped his hatbrim and smiled.

'Evening,' Kirby responded. 'How are you finding Macallister?'

'Extremely hospitable, Sheriff. I'm sure we're going to enjoy our stay here.'

'How long do you plan to be with us?' he asked.

'No telling, Sheriff. It depends on how our business progresses.'

'Well, I'm sure it will be successful,' Kirby said, sounding once again like the genuine article.

'Good night.'

'Good night, Sheriff.'

Kirby went to the doors and was reaching for the batwings when they opened and the fourth man of the party came through. He was very slender and sharp-faced and wore a six-shooter at his belt. For a moment the two paused, looking at one another. Kirby felt there might be something vaguely familiar about the fellow. But he couldn't place him, and when the man simply tugged at his hatbrim and stepped past, Kirby just shrugged and went out into the cool night.

He took the first side street to the open pastures that lay beyond and stood staring off at Crow Hill which appeared dark and deserted. Craig had taken him down there at dusk to show him over the mine. Kirby was impressed with the lengths they'd obviously gone to camouflage the workings. Unless a man knew there was something there he'd never know where to look for the cunningly concealed entrance in back of a bank of old cottonwoods.

The menfolk of the town worked the single narrow shaft nights. The silver was smelted underground and the bank arranged for its sale in Denver.

Kirby could easily understand why these people would want to keep the strike to themselves, yet still marvelled that so many had been able to keep the secret — until a certain drunk babbled one night in Helltown and the cat was out of the bag.

It was the thought of Helltown that turned his thoughts back to that slender man he'd encountered at the saloon a short time before. Had it been Helltown where he'd seen him? He couldn't be sure. Eventually he gave up, lit a cigar then set off on a patrol that would take him past the Craig house on Mount Street.

With luck, he might find Jade Craig on her stoop taking the evening air. With even more luck, she might invite him in for coffee. There was no telling how long it might be before he again shared the company of a real lady who seemed to like him.

If ever . . .

6

Gun Judgement

'I tell you I seen him in Helltown!' the hawk-faced Ketch insisted. 'He was with that Moss O'Shea and they was talkin' to that Pracy pilgrim. Pracy and Kirby had first met each other in the town square. It was on account old Moss seemed so interested in what Pracy was tellin' 'em that I got curious and had to go buy him a shot after they left. So that's how come *we* got to know about the silver. Savvy?'

Booth stared hard into Ketch's face for a long moment in total silence, his brain working overtime. He believed what he'd heard, for Ketch never made mistakes on important matters.

Booth had been proud of his original plan.

Faced with a choice between brains

or brute force to investigate Mace Pracy's drunken story of secret mines and huge wealth, Booth had finally plumped for brains.

He'd concocted a plan whereby a hired hard-case would go to Macallister, gun down the sheriff, raise general hell and plunge the whole community into a blue funk. Then, just as things were looking at their darkest for the town, along would come a powerful 'dealer' who would take the hell-raiser by the scruff and boot his ass all the way out of town.

The result?

Macallister would have an overnight hero in one Solway Booth, and from there on in it would only be a matter of time before they took him into their confidence and told him about their mine . . .

Sitting in his hotel room studying Ketch's sharp features, Booth still felt his plan had the stamp of real brilliance about it. Until it went wrong, of course. But who'd have anticipated Fabian losing a gunfight when he was regarded as next best to invincible?

Fabian had been gunned down by Kirby. Ketch claimed he was an O'Shea man, and yet he wore Macallister's star.

The longer he considered this the more it appeared certain that O'Shea was hard at work with his own plans to plunder the Macallister cache, now well advanced.

Booth's smooth face was expressionless as he rose and poured a stiff double shot. Then he remembered he didn't drink. He stared around the room at the silent men. Was he showing signs of being rattled? He shook his head. No. Not him. Not cool-headed Solway Booth.

'I believe you, Ketch,' he said calmly. 'Kirby killed Fabian and they made him their sheriff because of that. O'Shea must be laughing fit to kill to think they'd make it easy for him. With one of his gunmen wearing the star in town he must calculate it's only one short step from marching off with the big take.'

'What big take, boss?' Wannamaker asked. 'We've took a good look around this dump and we ain't seen hide nor hair of no minin' operation.'

'It's here,' Booth declared. 'I can smell it!'

Nobody argued. Booth was never wrong about such matters. He had a nose for nubile women and easy money that was infallible.

'So, where do we go from here, Solway?' Jackson asked, watching the street from the window.

'First things first,' Booth replied briskly. 'We don't know what O'Shea's full strength is, but this Kirby has to be his ace.' The pince-nez reflected the light as he glanced around. 'Kirby's got to go. Now!'

* * *

The town clock showed a little after ten. Kirby watched it through a haze of cigar smoke from the jailhouse porch. Another hour and he'd saddle up to go meet one of the boys out by Buzzard Butte to report on his progress.

O'Shea would be tickled pink when he learned he'd been successful in landing the lawman's job. Kirby didn't expect it would take O'Shea long to figure out a plan involving Sheriff Kirby and Macallister's pile of silver. Success surely would only be a matter of time. He wondered if Moss would vote him a bonus for playing the key role in the big operation?

Unlikely, he mused, flicking the stogie away as he went down the steps. Should anybody draw an extra cut, it would most likely be Moss himself . . .

Macallister was still noisy as he set out on his patrol. Music spilled from the open windows of Fat Libby's and the Diamondback, and he heard a woman singing, punctuated by the occasional burst of laughter.

He went on down past the darkened front of the billiard parlour, the general store, then on past the lamplit landing of the stage depot — suddenly conscious of a strange feeling inside. It was as though he was a real sheriff and Macallister was the town he must protect!

'*Sheriff!*'

He propped and turned. A man stood in the alley which ran between the feed and grain barn and the blacksmith's. The man beckoned. Kirby recognized him by his pince-nez. The one named Smith.

'What is it, Mr Smith?'

Booth gestured at the alley. 'There's a drunken man down there who attempted to rob me.'

Reaching the alley mouth, Kirby peered along the gloomy corridor to detect a weaving, tattered figure waving a bottle. As the drunk burst into song he realized it was Rumpot Jake.

It passed through his mind that it was odd that a rumpot like Jake would attempt robbery then loiter around afterwards as if just waiting to be nabbed.

But he was the sheriff, a complaint had been made, and there could be no doubting that Rumpot was guilty of drunkenness, at least.

With a nod to Booth he started off down the alley. Rumpot waved his bottle at the moon and ripped off a stanza of the Confederate Marching Song. The singing broke off as he walked into a paling fence. The man was drunk as a fiddler's cat, and Lee Kirby had no way of suspecting that he'd been treated to free whiskey for the past hour to get him into that condition.

Rumpot! Why the hell didn't he stay in bed?

The drunk turned. Kirby reached for him. But as he did Solway Booth's booming shout shattered the night.

'Sheriff! Don't shoot him!'

Kirby whirled. As he did, the alleyway rocked to the blast of a .45. Kirby threw himself headlong and whipped out his six-shooter with blinding speed.

Booth had dived from sight. Lee's head rang from the gunshot but he wasn't hit. A gurgling sound close by caused him to twist his head, his eyes jolting wide in shock. Rumpot Jake lay against the base of the fence with his body twisted at an unnatural angle.

Kirby heard the stutter of running feet from an empty building close by. Springing erect, he streaked for the building but slowed when he heard shouting from Trail Street and Booth's voice again.

'Don't go in there, men. It's the sheriff. He must have gone kill-crazy! He just gunned down an old drunk in cold blood!'

Kirby's scalp pulled tight. What in the name of Judas was going on here?

He spun back to Rumpot Jake and dropped to one knee at his side. He felt for a heartbeat. There wasn't one. The drunk had been shot through the chest.

'There he is, boys! Be careful, he's still got a gun!'

Coming erect in one oiled motion,

Kirby saw the alleymouth now crowded with drinkers from the saloons. He holstered his Colt and the panic began to recede. He strode out into Trail Street looking for the man in the pince-nez. He sighted him standing in front of the store, but he was now flanked by two of his men, the scar-faced felon and the giant with the broad shoulders.

The big man moved aggressively forward as Kirby shouldered a towner aside and headed for his accuser.

'Grab hold of him, you men!' the giant bawled. 'He looks mad enough to kill again!'

'I didn't kill anybody,' Kirby raged. 'Smith, you're lying. You know I didn't fire a shot!'

Suddenly, somebody began shouting from the alley. 'It's Rumpot Jake, and he's as dead as mutton!'

'They were wrangling,' Booth told the mob. 'The sheriff lost his temper, drew his gun and shot him down. It was terrible!'

Kirby lunged at his accuser. But Wannamaker shouldered him off balance. Suddenly, Mitch Craig burst out of the mob, face pale with shock and alarm.

'Lee, what in God's name happened here?'

Kirby attempted to explain but too many people were talking at once.

'Why would these men lie, Kirby?' the blacksmith demanded. 'Mebbe we should have known you was just a killer after the way you shot down Fabian.'

'Butcher!' another man bawled. Then a saloon girl cried out, 'Lock him up in his own cells. He ain't a lawman, he's a killer!'

'Better give me your gun until we find out what this is all about, Lee,' Craig advised as the swelling crowd began closing in. He yelled, 'Back off, you men. I can handle this!'

'You made him sheriff and it was a dirty mistake, Craig!' bellowed a tottering drunk. 'B'God, jailin' him is too good for what he done, I reckon. Why don't somebody git a rope?'

Kirby felt the chill of alarm. The dealer and his men had done such an artful job of whipping up the half-drunk saloon boozers that they were now in a genuinely dangerous frame of mind. A mob in that mood was capable of anything.

In one fluid motion he drew his .45 and sprang back away from them.

'Hold up!' he almost snarled. 'This here is nothing but a dirty frame. But I doubt that I can prove that to you right now.'

He jabbed an accusing finger at Booth.

'That man set me up. Don't ask me why, but he did. And I reckon he knows who gunned old Rumpot. But I can't prove that here and I'm not waiting around for a bunch of fools and drunks to string me up. And seeing as I don't want to kill anybody, I'm leaving. But if anyone tries to stop me, I swear I'll cut loose.'

They started yelling, but broke off

when Kirby drilled a shot just over their heads. He was backing up another pace when Booth hollered, 'Are you just going to stand there and let a cold-blooded killer escape?'

'No chance of that,' came a voice from directly behind him, and Kirby whirled to see a glittering six-gun trained upon him from a gap in the bakery door.

'Freeze, Kirby!' the invisible gunman bawled.

It was a desperate moment for Lee Kirby. He knew now he'd been set up as neatly and cleverly as any man had ever been. Yet angry as he was, he was still loath to start in shooting. There was no guessing how many might die should gunplay erupt. But how could any man simply allow himself to be taken and likely lynched ? He could not do that. He trained his gun muzzle on the bakery door. He was ready to cut loose.

But he didn't.

'*Lee!*'

Her voice reached him clearly. She moved into his line of vision from the right, small and fragile-looking in the moonlight with hands clasping a knit shawl about her shoulders.

'Lee — please don't kill anyone else!'

'Anyone *else*?' His voice was hoarse with impotent anger. 'I haven't killed anybody goddamnit — '

He broke off as a heavy hand fell upon his shoulder from behind. He twisted to stare into Craig's face.

'Hand me the Colt, Lee. You have my word no harm will come to you. I know these people and I can control them, but only if you give up your gun.'

'The safest place for you now will be in jail, Lee,' Jade said. 'Please do it for me?'

Suddenly he was drained of all energy. If he were to start in shooting he'd be risking her life and her father's. He'd fallen for a sucker play and figured he might be lucky to get out of it alive. Yet even so he was still not prepared to usher in wholesale slaughter by using his gun . . .

The mob fell strangely silent as he handed Jade his weapon. Her presence, Kirby's surrender, and Craig's guarantee of safety seemed to have taken the mob off the boil. And the man with the pince-nez now seemed content and made no further move to incite them.

'Thank you, Lee,' Jade said softly, but scarce anybody heard.

'Come on then,' Craig said, signalling to councillors to move in and form an escort.

They held his arms as they led him away.

★ ★ ★

Rolfe had ridden steadily from Bracken Canyon. It was eleven o'clock when he arrived at the rendezvous at Buzzard Butte. There was no sign of Kirby. He got down and watered his horse at the little spring, then rolled a cigarette and smoked it through.

Still no sign.

He went to his saddle-bags and broke out a flagon of sourmash. It was a fine moonlight night and he could think of many worse things to be doing than enjoying the peace and quiet with a bottle while dreaming about rivers of silver and the luxury of life in Old Mexico.

By midnight he was a worried man, by one o'clock he knew something had gone wrong. Kirby had not been with the bunch long but Rolfe knew he was reliable.

On impulse he clambered halfway up the flank of the butte and gazed towards the far off lights of Macallister for another half-hour without sighting any sign of life.

He could not hang about any longer. Returning to his horse, he tightened up the cinch, climbed into the saddle. And dug heel.

★　★　★

Jackson chuckled as he thumbed the cork out of his bottle.

124

'It was so damn easy,' he chortled. 'Hell, why didn't we blast him while we was at it? We'd be all done with him now.'

'If you'll recall, hardcase,' Solway Booth said with heavy irony, 'you all voted just to take him out of the game — not bury him. You were, I believe, heavily influenced in your decision by what had happened to Fabian, who was faster than any of you on the best day you ever had.'

Jackson opened his mouth to argue but thought better of it. For Booth was only speaking the simple truth. Before the drama of Trail Street, all of them had been in a cold sweat about the risk involved in tackling Kirby.

'The boss man's right,' Ketch declared, toying with the Colt that had blasted Rumpot Jake into the next world. 'It's more fun drillin' drunk old fellers than hardnoses who might just start shootin' back if you don't get 'em first shot.'

'You handled your part well, Ketch,'

Booth said quietly. 'You're the top gun now Fabian's gone.'

Ketch looked proud. He liked the sound of that. He had always wanted to be top gun.

'It was easy, boss,' he said modestly, housing the weapon. 'Well, who's next?'

'Nobody just yet, I hope,' Booth replied, neatly slicing the top off his breakfast egg with a big steel knife. He examined the contents, found them to be satisfactory, applied salt and pepper. He smiled.

'By the time I get through with Craig and his yellow-guts councillors today I'll have them believing I saved them all from somebody who's a cross between Khan and Quantrell — '

'Who?' Wannamaker asked.

'Hush up and let Sol get on with it,' Jackson said.

'So,' Booth continued, 'I'll have them eating out of my hand. Exactly as I would've done if my first plan with Fabian had panned out.' He spread his hands. 'And the result should be the same. Once they're convinced I'm the holy saviour come to help them and the sort of pard you couldn't buy with gold, it'll only be a matter of time before I find out where their mine's located.'

'If there is one,' Wannamaker muttered.

'There is,' Booth said with conviction, and attacked his egg once again.

'Time,' Ketch mused thoughtfully from the window. 'That's all right so long as we got plenty of it . . . '

'Meaning?' Booth was sharp.

'Meaning if this Kirby is still with O'Shea, like we figure, then old Moss might make a sudden move that'll catch us on the hop. Leastwise that's how I see it.'

Booth was not annoyed by the statement, and even looked pleased as he rose, dabbing at his lips.

'Excellent, Ketch, excellent. It shows that at least one of you is thinking ahead.'

He crossed to the bureau and began putting on his necktie. He'd already been shaved and Jackson was busily polishing his pince-nez for him with a twist of paper.

'I considered that very possibility when making my plans for Kirby just last night. And it helped me reach the decision to have Kirby put out of the way rather than killed.'

He turned to face them with the tie perfectly knotted.

'You see, Kirby alive is another string to our bow — providing I make the progress I expect with Craig.'

'I don't figure what you're sayin', boss,' Ketch scowled. 'You want to explain some?'

Booth took his pince-nez and set them upon his nose, just so. Then he slipped into the jacket Jackson held for him and buttoned it neatly across his waistcoat.

'Kirby's in a desperate situation,' he stated. 'He wants out. And I could arrange for him to get out, providing he made it worth my while. And just how might he do that? There is no way . . . unless he already knows what we want to hear about the silver.' He smiled smugly. 'Get the drift now, boys?'

They got it. Even big, dumb Wannamaker who chuckled admiringly.

'You sure as hell wasn't left standin' behind the door when they handed out the brains, boss. When you goin' to quiz him?'

'After I've seen Craig,' Booth replied, scooping up his hat. 'Ketch, I want you to go to the jail and make sure Kirby's being securely guarded.'

'Sure thing, Solway.'

'What about me and Jackson, boss?' Wannamaker wanted to know. 'What you want us to do?'

Booth's smooth face was sober as he went to the door. 'You keep an eye out for Moss O'Shea. If he shows his hand too soon, all my plans could come to nothing and it could end up like hell with all the fences down.'

This was a sobering thought yet the outlaws weren't overly impressed. They still hoped to relieve Macallister of its silver the easy way if things went according to Booth's planning, but they were prepared to win the hard way if they must.

Booth smiled genially at the woman at the hotel desk on his stately way out and she was deeply impressed.

'Such a fine gentleman,' she told the porter. 'And such a brave one too, standing up to Sheriff Kirby the way he did last night.'

'We need more like him in Macallister,' the porter agreed. 'Mr Smith strikes me as just the sort of strong man and leader we've been missin' ever since Mayor Hinch was killed. Wonder if him and his pards plan on stayin'?'

That same question was raised during Booth's lengthy discussion with Mayor Craig and Banker Swan over beers and a mineral water at Fat Libby's later that morning. Booth made sure it was raised while playing out his role as a potential permanent Macallister resident for all it was worth.

He let the citizens know that he'd come to their town looking for the right location to set up a permanent agency, and felt Macallister to be just the place. But, of course, there were reservations. It wasn't so much the violence he objected to but he wasn't sure he could live with all the secrecy.

'Secrecy?' Craig and Swan said together. 'What secrecy?'

Booth appeared distressed to think they thought he was not quick and smart enough to realize Macallister was nursing a big secret.

'Of course, any town has a perfect right to its secrets — but there are good secrets and bad secrets. Before I even considered putting my roots down here — or started bringing in a flood of new business — I'd have to know in what category your secrets might be . . . '

They didn't cave in and confess their secrets right then and there — and he hardly expected them to. Yet they did hint he might be right about Macallister and that they might consider becoming more frank with him at a later date, should he elect to become a permanent citizen.

Booth didn't allow his disappointment to show. He glanced at the bar clock, mindful of what Ketch had said earlier about time. He was certain he could con these stiff-necked hicks into opening up and spilling their insides, given time. Yet he dare not gamble on the time factor.

He decided to check on his men then pay a call on ex-Sheriff Kirby . . .

7

One More Grave

He'd never been in jail before.

There had been wild brawls, midnight chases, shady deals and high-stake gambling games that often exploded into outright violence when someone turned out to be a sore loser. Yet through all the high times and hell-raising he'd somehow always managed to stay clear of prison.

Until now.

Kirby was attempting to recall some of those sad, romantic poems about prison life as he first stared up at this narrow barred window, but they wouldn't come to him. The voices from the front office kept intruding. His jailers were swilling coffee and loudly discussing his prospects when he faced judge and jury; they seemed to be in

133

agreement that he would swing.

A bitter smile twisted his mouth as he slouched to the barred door and leaned against it. Macallister appeared to have found its grit and gumption at exactly the wrong time.

The face of the man who called himself Smith floated before his eyes. He'd been given ample time to think things over, and there was no doubt in his mind that the four newcomers were outlaws of the most desperate stamp. They'd taken him off the streets because he was the law, and it had to be obvious now that in doing so they planned to clear the way for a crime. Following this notion through to its natural conclusion, he could think only of the silver lying in the bank vault — and that little mine below Crow Hill.

He'd passed on his suspicions to Mitch Craig, of course, yet doubted it had been worth the effort. Craig was a confused man. All Macallister seemed confused, yet their one overriding belief seemed to be that he was guilty of murder. The bastards were at least clear about that.

Smoke hung in grey tatters about his face as he lit up a cigar. Inhaling deeply, he leaned his muscular back against the bars and thought long and hard on how he might alert Moss O'Shea of his plight. Until a light step and a waft of subtle scent heralded his first visitor of the day.

He slowly drew his stogie from his lips and stared at Jade Craig through the bars. She appeared pale and drawn and he was certain she hadn't rested. But she still looked pretty with her hair drawn back from her face and wearing a blouse of a colour that matched her eyes.

'Hello, Lee.'

'Howdy.'

'Are you all right?'

'Never better. You?'

'I'm fine.'

'We're both pretty lousy liars, aren't we?'

She drew closer, eyes scanning his

face. 'I haven't slept a wink, Lee, I — '

'Kinda figured that. Well, I gotta be honest and allow I didn't get much shut-eye myself.'

She hesitated, then said clearly, 'I . . . I believe you.'

'What?'

'I've gone over and over everything that was said and done in my mind, and I just know you didn't kill Jake.'

He grinned for the first time in many a long hour. 'Well, that's something, I can tell you. And I'm glad you came to see me, girl, even if it won't do either of us one lick of good.'

'I've tried to convince Dad you're simply incapable of murder, but he keeps arguing that there are four witnesses who say you did it.'

'Mr Smith and his dealers. Well, I've tried to convince everybody that they're a bunch of killers, liars and scum but they just won't swallow it. I guess Smith's simply too good an actor.'

'Lee — what'll happen to you?'

'Depends.'

'On what?'

'On whether I escape or not.'

Her eyes widened. 'Can you escape? I mean — '

'Not without help. I don't suppose you'd like to help . . . seeing as you don't believe I did it?'

'I don't understand. How could I help?'

He studied her intently, an idea rapidly forming in his mind. He was reluctant to involve her — yet was even more reluctant to stand by helplessly while Smith and his cohorts played out their ugly game.

'Can I trust you, Jade?'

'To do what?'

'To keep whatever I might tell you to yourself?'

'Of course.'

He knew he had to believe that. 'All right then. The truth is — I'm not alone.'

'What do you mean?'

'I've got friends who'd get me out of here if they knew what was going on.'

'What kind of . . . friends? Where are they?'

'You know Bracken Canyon?' She nodded and he went on. 'They're out there waiting for me. They're wolvers and good men. Honest. If you were to ride out there and tell them what's happened, Jade, Moss would figure out some way to help me.'

'I wonder why I want to say yes when I know I should refuse?'

'My charm?' He tried to make a joke of it but it didn't come off.

'I simply can't sit back and see you suffer for something I know you couldn't do, Lee,' Jade said gravely. 'I'll go to Bracken Canyon if you give me your word no harm will come to Macallister as a result.'

Kirby realized he must be getting too soft for his own good because he was finding it increasingly difficult to lie.

Yet he still managed it.

'You have my word,' he muttered, not looking at her. There was a long silence. He finally glanced up to see her staring at him. 'Well, what do you want?' he said gruffly. 'You want it signed in blood?'

'I'll go immediately, Lee,' she said quietly, moving off. 'Do please take care.'

He lifted his hand, and framed the words to call her back. But she was already gone.

* * *

'Ashes to ashes and dust to dust,' the preacher intoned. 'May you take him to your bosom, oh Lord, and if it's not asking too much — please see to it that he doesn't go too thirsty.'

Religion was more than just words in a book and sore knees from the praying for Preacher Flynn. A man with a powerful fondness for the bottle himself, he could sympathize with someone like Rumpot Jake who might feel the need of something stronger than pearls of dew and angel tears when and if he ever made it to paradise.

'The Lord giveth and the Lord taketh away . . .'

A sizeable crowd had turned up to bid farewell to Macallister's most dedicated and likeable drunk. Mitch Craig was among the mourners but was not concentrating on the service as he stood, hands clasped before him, staring over the bowed heads at the distant squat bulk of Crow Hill.

Craig didn't know how exactly, yet he was totally convinced that silver lay behind the sudden plague of violence that had engulfed his town with the ferocity of a Texas twister.

In his early days as a cub reporter in Chicago his boozy old city editor had instructed him, 'Whenever trouble breaks, always look for the dame or the dough.'

According to Craig's former mentor, ninety-five per cent of all man's troubles sprang either from women or wealth. Craig refused to believe that even a wagonload of wild women from Storeyville could cause as much bloodshed as Macallister had seen that week — so that only left the money.

The silver.

Macallister's secret.

Craig had always been a strong supporter of the town's decision to continue working the Crow Hill vein, share the profits, and keep its existence a secret amongst themselves. He'd seen so much good come from that silver. Yet he was beginning to believe the good days were drawing to an end. He'd thought it all through and was convinced that the late Mace Pracy had spilled the secret after being banished from Macallister . . .

With a start, Craig realized the service had come to an end. Mourners were already leaving for town by foot, horseback or buggy. He went with them, but his thoughts remained behind at Crow Hill. Something would have to be done about the mine if further trouble was to be avoided, he assured himself. But what? He shook his head. He didn't know. He was a newspaperman, not Solomon.

★   ★   ★

Solway Booth placed the office chair in the corridor, directly before the cell door. He sat down upon it, crossed his legs, adjusted the seams of his immaculate trousers, then removed his hard-hitter hat and sat it upon his knee, just so.

The pince-nez shone with a brilliance as he looked at the towners who'd escorted him into the cells.

'It's perfectly safe to leave me alone, my friends,' he assured them all. 'I have nothing to fear from the prisoner.' He paused to smile at Lee. 'Do I, Kirby?'

There was no response from the prisoner. The towners exchanged glances and shrugs before silently returning to the front office.

'Fine men, Kirby, salt of the earth. You mustn't hold it against them just because they might be reacting badly to one of their own being cut down in such a brutal fashion. They're simple people. Not like you and me, huh? We're a different breed — right?'

'I reckon I got your breed figured pretty damn good by this. You're a cold-blooded, butcherin' outlaw son of a bitch. Correct?'

The smooth face beamed tolerantly.

'Ahh, you're outspoken and impetuous, Kirby, like most young men?' The smile vanished. 'Who are you, mister? Your name, I mean. I know you're one of Moss O'Shea's lapdogs.'

Kirby could not hide his surprise.

'Who's O'Shea?'

'Who is he? Why, a broken-down nobody who's got the notion he's somebody all of a sudden. If that wasn't so then he wouldn't be horning in on this affair which is so obviously too big for his limited talents to cope with. Would he?'

'Moss might have his drawbacks, but at least he don't go round murderin' old drunks in back alleys.'

'No, he leaves that to his underlings. You. They'll hang you, Kirby. You know that, don't you?'

'I reckon not. To hang me they'd have to try me first. And to get a conviction the 'eye witness' would have to appear. Somehow I can't picture you or your scum showin' up within fifty miles of any courthouse, Smith. You wouldn't dare. So, what's your next shot?'

'You're smart, Kirby, smart enough. And you're right, of course. If they don't lynch you in the meantime you'll be set free through lack of evidence. But of course, that's looking into the future, isn't it? By the time all that has come to pass the situation here will have been resolved, one way or another.'

'Meanin'?'

'Meaning the silver, of course, Kirby. Where the hell is it?'

Lee turned his back and moved across to the window. That little square of blue sky meant a great deal to him.

He wanted to be riding free under a Colorado sky so badly that he was even prepared to use a girl he thought highly of to help him achieve his goal.

It was galling to think of Smith and his dog pack having free access to that wide world . . .

He turned his head. 'Pracy?'

'Why beat about the bush, Kirby? Of course it was Pracy.'

'Did you kill him afterwards?'

'No, he managed to get himself killed. So, now that we have cleared the air why don't we get right down to the nugget of things, Kirby? Tell me about the silver and I'll see to it that you're set free.'

'How can you do that without admittin' you lied about the killin' last night?'

'There are always ways and means for a man willing to use his brains. Rest assured, I can get you out of it if we strike a bargain.'

Kirby walked back to the door and clutched the bars.

'What if I said there ain't any silver?'

'I'd say you were lying.'

'Why?'

'Macallister's plainly richer than any regular cattle town and its citizens are nursing some big secret — that sticks out a mile. The mathematics of that adds up to the fact that Pracy told the truth about a hidden silver mine.'

'You're right, of course.'

Booth leaned forward eagerly. 'I goddamn knew it! Where is it, man?'

'First, let me hear how you'll bust me out.'

'I'll go straight to Craig and the others, of course. I'll tell them I've suffered agonies of conscience, that I'm no longer certain what I saw in that alley.'

'They won't swallow that.'

'I'll guarantee they will.'

'Well, go try it. You get me out and I'll tell you all you want to know about the mine.'

'Ahh no, I don't trust you that far,

Kirby. First the information — then I go to work.

Kirby laughed in his face. 'You reckon I'd trust the word of a low-life son of a bitch who'd murder an old man just to get an advantage over me?'

Booth rose, pale-faced now. 'You're playing with death, you realize, outlaw? If I was to whip these people up into a frenzy and pump them up with free liquor I could get them to drag you outside and hang you from the nearest tree. I'm a mighty persuasive speaker . . . as you likely observed last night.'

'Go fry, Smith. I'd rather burn in hell than do any kind of deal with you.'

Booth carefully fitted his hat to his head, his face cold. 'Very well, Kirby, I'll go. But I'll be back. You won't walk so tall when you get your first smell of that hemp rope.'

Lee laughed scornfully as Booth left — but was far from laughing inside. He hoped to hell Jade hadn't let him down.

8

Ride Every Trail

They weren't wolf hunters.

Jade was sure of this by the time the red-headed man with the vicious scar down one side of his face had escorted her to the cabin where another four men waited, each gun-hung and stone-faced in the sunlight.

There were no skins or traps, no sign that honest work of any kind was being carried out here at Bracken Canyon. Her throat felt very dry as the oldest of the bunch, a strange-looking man with yellow eyes, motioned to her to step down. Quite suddenly she sensed that men who looked and acted this way could only be outlaws.

And they weren't Lee's friends . . .

'Flint tells me you're lookin' for Lee's pards, little lady,' Moss O'Shea growled, jerking a thumb at the red-headed man who'd brought her to the camp. 'Well, here we are. So, what's goin' on?'

Jade mustered her strength before responding in short, concise sentences. She watched their glances harden as they learned that Lee was in jail and that his situation could only be described as desperate.

When she was through the bunch withdrew out of earshot to confer in low tones together. The older man did most of the talking and it was he who led the bunch back to her, nodding his grizzled head.

'All right, you done good bringin' us this message, little lady. We'll take care of things from here on in.'

'You'll help Lee?'

'Of course. We're his pards, ain't we? But afore you leave, lady, I'm mighty curious about this here Smith pilgrim you told us about. I'd kinda like you to describe him to us.'

Jade obliged — and Moss O'Shea

suddenly twitched as though stung. '*Booth*!' he hissed. 'Solway goddamn Booth! That tricky, double-dealin' son of a whoremaster!'

He broke off with a sucked intake of breath, jabbed a finger at the girl. 'How many has this pilgrim got with him in your town, lady?'

'Three. Why, do you know him?'

'That sure ain't no concern of yours,' came the brooding reply. 'But, like I say, you done real good. Now you can vamoose and leave the rest to us.'

Although her mind was buzzing with things she wanted to ask — mostly about Lee — Jade was only too ready to mount and ride. These men made her very nervous, apart from the quiet-voiced one with the dark moustache called Joe who came to hold her horse's head as he called back to the leader.

'I'll escort Miss Craig back to the trail, pard. Ain't safe for any gal riding alone in this kind of country.'

'Then make it goddamn snappy,' O'Shea growled. 'Lee expects us to help him and we don't have time to waste.'

The man with the moustache grunted and went to get to his horse. Falling in at Jade's side he gave her a reassuring smile and they rode out together. As Jade hipped around in the saddle for a final glance she saw the men standing in a huddle, talking intensely. She looked a question at her escort.

'Guess you're kind of curious about us, eh, Miss Craig? Maybe we ain't exactly what you expected?'

They crested a rise, then the camp dropped from sight behind.

'Lee told me you were hunters,' she said, 'but you're really not, are you?'

'Maybe not. But he was right about us bein' his friends. We'll prise him loose of that jail even if we got to fill their graveyard doin' it.'

All colour fled from the girl's shocked face. 'What on earth do you mean?'

'Miss Craig, I guess Lee figgered he couldn't be honest with you about who he is and what we are, otherwise you mightn't have brought us his message. But now you've done what he wanted I reckon there ain't much to lose and maybe somethin' to gain by being a little more candid mebbe.'

'Are you . . . are you outlaws?'

'Let's just say we ain't no better than we should be. All of us but Lee, that is. Seein' as you think high of that boy, I got to tell you that he ain't stamped with the same brand as the rest of us, girl. He's only been with us a short spell and I've had the notion all along he shouldn't ought to be ridin' with us at all. I guess he just got wearied of tryin' to make somethin' of hisself the slow and hard way, and decided he'd try our way instead. This here is Lee's first job.'

'Job?' Jade stumbled on the word.

'Was to be, leastwise. But, you know, mebbe there's still time to stop this goin' that far — which is somethin' I see in your face. You could likely help him, iffen you wanted to.'

'I don't understand what you're implying.'

The man guided his mount around a rocky outcropping and squinted ahead at the line of trees marking the high trail.

'Moss — that's the boss man back there — will bust Lee out, Miss Craig, on account Lee knows where your mine's located. That'll make him as guilty as the rest of us — and it'll be plain too late for him then.'

It took Jade some time to absorb what Joe was saying. She felt dazed, yet even so was aware that this new knowledge seemed to have little effect upon her feelings towards Lee if any.

She'd felt from the very start there was something mysterious and possibly dangerous about him, so discovering he was part of an outlaw band didn't come as great a shock as it might have done.

Yet she did find herself clinging desperately to Joe's insistence that Lee wasn't daubed with the same brush as himself and the others. If Lee hadn't actually broken the law, then there could still be hope.

Yet still the biggest challenge was to get him out of that jail first — and without bloodshed.

She said, 'What can we do, Joe? I can't stand by and let innocent people get hurt when your men come to Macallister. I'd have to warn them.'

They'd reached the trail by this. Joe Rolfe reined in before an old cottonwood and fingered back his hat before dipping fingers into a pocket. Jade stared at the odd-looking wire-and-metal gadget he brought forth. Rolfe flipped it over a couple of times then closed his fingers over it and looked up at her.

'I'm the lock-picker and safe-cracker in this bunch out here, Miss Craig.'

He opened his fingers.

'This here's a skeleton key I made that'll open any lock ever made.' He passed it to her. 'Slip that to Lee and he'll do the rest. And tell him Joe Rolfe said that as soon as he's out he's to disappear. Warn him to get you and him to hell and gone out of town and leave Booth and us to fight over the silver. Tell him . . . ahh, I'm just wasting time. I figure a fine, level-headed gal like you can figure out what to tell him yourself. Will you do it?'

'Yes I will, Joe,' she replied without hesitation. She studied the contraption in her hand. 'Why didn't you get your friends to get Lee out of jail?'

'I don't want me or the boys to have nothin' to do with Lee gettin' out. I don't want him to feel obligated to us none.'

'Why are you doing this for Lee, Joe?'

He looked away.

'I was like Lee Kirby once, Miss Craig.' He nodded. 'Uh-huh, that's his rightful full name. Lee Kirby from Catamount County. Well, I was twenty-five and gettin' too greedy for my own good, so I took what I figured to be the easy way. Now I'm a beat-up outlaw with holes in my boots and maybe not all that far from the Misty Beyond.'

He paused and gave a wintry smile.

'I'm thirty-three years old and feel seventy-three. I never met a gal like you who was ready to take every damnfool risk in the book to help me. Mebbe if I had, things might've been different. But Lee's still got a chance to step back from the brink, and now it's up to you to see he grabs it. That's if you care enough, of course.' A pause. 'Do you?'

'I . . . I think I do.'

'Then get ridin', miss. And . . . and if anythin' should happen and I don't get to see you or Lee again, I'd like you to think that maybe you might give me a kind thought now and again. Reckon you could do that?'

Jade swallowed the lump in her throat, realizing with sudden clarity that the quiet-voiced outlaw was talking about death.

'I'll do everything you say, Joe.' She reached for his hand. 'Goodbye.'

'*Adios*, Miss Craig. I guess it'd be too much to ask you not to warn your town that we'll be comin' in?'

'I'm afraid that would be asking too much, Joe.'

He smiled sadly.

'Sure it would. Well, you just do what you got to, but make sure you and Lee get out of town no matter what. There ain't goin' to be no stoppin' Moss now, and there never was any stoppin' Solway Booth. Like the good book says, missy, there's goin' to be 'lions in the streets' before this day's over.'

He swung away and rode off through the trees to be swallowed swiftly from sight. With heart in her mouth, Jade touched her horse's flanks with spurs and pointed its head for home.

★ ★ ★

Within an hour of the wire reaching Mitch Craig's desk at the *Courier* office, its contents were common knowledge. In response to the mayor's wire for assistance in light of the recent spate of killings in Macallister, the

Villanova marshal's office had dispatched three marshals to investigate the troubles and take charge of the prisoner — former sheriff Lee Kirby.

The wire came as a big relief to Mitch Craig who was feeling worn and drained by recent events, in particular the murder of Rumpot Jake and Kirby's arrest. Tempers had cooled, but Craig would still be a happy man to hand over the responsibilities to men more qualified to handle them.

The news had a significantly different effect on Solway Booth. Ever since turning the tables on Kirby and emerging from the Rumpot Jake affair as a solid, reliable citizen, Booth had been attempting to winkle out the location of the mine from Craig and the others — but without success.

The realization that lawmen would be arriving within the next forty-eight hours threw Booth's henchmen into something close to panic, yet Booth himself remained cool. He was still committed to using his brain to achieve success. He would continue to work on Craig and the others while his men were ordered to keep eyes and ears open for any hint of a clue to the mine's whereabouts. They still had time, he told them, and they would make the most of it.

'What if we still ain't no closer to flushin' this goddamn mine by this time tomorrow, Solway?' big Wannamaker growled. 'Will we take the gloves off then?'

'We'll have no choice, will we?'

Wannamaker looked reassured. Leaning back in his saloon chair he cracked his knuckles in anticipation of taking off the gloves. Then all four drank a toast — in lemon juice — to their eventual success. Booth was so determined to come out on top he'd placed a ban on all booze until they rode out of Macallister with the silver.

Which was an easy enough law to lay down for a man who never touched the stuff.

Night in Macallister.

Kirby stood by his cell window watching the stars appear. A cigar angled from his lips and his muscular body was relaxed as he listened to the piano music flowing from the opened windows of the Diamondback saloon. Upon the stool by his door were the remains of the evening meal, brought in by Kentucky Phil just on dusk.

Phil's meals were an improvement upon those he served in his eatery next door. The hash house proprietor was one of those who refused to believe that Kirby had killed the old drunk, and was intent on easing his lot with the best available chow.

He turned his head at the sound of steps to see the liveryman, Race Thompson, appear at his door.

'Visitor for you, Kirby.' The liveryman's tone was sharp. He enjoyed playing jailer. 'You want to see her?'

'Her?'

'Miss Jade.'

'Show her in.'

Relief flooded Lee's face as he waited by the door. It had been a long afternoon. He heard her light step and then she was standing before him, eyes appearing greener than ever in the lantern light.

'I'd sooner you didn't stand too close to the door, Miss Jade,' the liveryman advised. 'Just to be on the safe side, you understand?'

Obligingly, Jade stepped back a pace. The man grunted in satisfaction and tramped back down the passageway, jingling his keys like a genuine turnkey.

'Well, Jade?' Kirby said softly.

She nodded. 'I saw your friends. They're coming to get you out.'

'That's a big one I owe you. Did they say how they plan to do it?'

'Joe Rolfe said it would be the hard way.'

Kirby's eyes snapped wide. 'How'd you know that name?'

'Joe told me himself.' She made a small gesture.

'We can drop the pretences, Lee. The moment I first saw your friends, I knew who they were.'

He sighed. 'Reckoned you might.' He shrugged. 'So, now you know girl. Where does that leave us now?'

'That depends.'

'On what?'

'I can get you out of here — before your friends show up. But before I do that I want to know what you'll do if I help you escape. Joe urged you to leave Macallister and take me with you before the trouble starts. He said, 'There'll be lions in the streets' — they were his exact words.'

Kirby nodded. That sounded like Joe Rolfe right enough. 'I'm sorry I couldn't level with you about what I am but I figured that if I did you wouldn't help me. I can't figure you still offerin' to help me now you've read my brand, though.'

'I think it's because I see more in you

162

than you see in yourself,' she replied calmly. 'Joe told me this was to be your first job. I'd like it to be also your last. In fact, I'd like you to forget the whole thing entirely. So, if I help you escape, will you just forget all about the silver? Agree to make a fresh start some place else?'

He was surprised just how easy it was to answer.

'Not only willin' but eager, Jade,' he grinned. 'So, some outlaw I turned out to be. But — hell! I knew I was sick of that life even before I got started!'

She smiled for the first time since her arrival.

'I just hoped and prayed you might say that, Lee.' She glanced towards the front, then opened her purse. Taking something out, she passed it quickly through the bars to him then stepped back again. Opening his hand, Kirby stared down at a strange-looking object which somehow looked vaguely familiar.

'What — ?'

'Joe gave me that. He called it a skeleton key, said it will unlock any door.'

Kirby stared wonderingly at the metal piece, raised his gaze to the girl. 'You'd best leave. I'll give you time to get back home before I try this thing out. If I can get out without rousin' the whole town, I'll come back to the house inside the half-hour. You'll leave with me?'

'I-I don't know . . . '

'Why not?'

'Lee, this is my town and it's in great danger from your friends — and with that Solway Booth about — '

'Solway Booth?'

'Your friends told me that's who Smith is when I described him to them. Do you know that name, Lee?'

'I surely do. He's one of the biggest outlaws in the South. But surely your knowin' that is all the more reason for you to quit town with me, Jade? It'll be pure hell if Moss comes to town and locks horns with Booth.'

'I shall have to alert Dad to the danger, Lee. Macallister will need to be prepared to defend itself. Some of your friends could even die.'

His face was grim. 'You've got to do what you've got to do, Jade.'

'You don't care?'

'I had a lot of time to think. About my life and the fool thing I did lookin' for quick success on the owlhoot. I was through with that life even before you walked in, Jade. I'd already made up my mind that whatever happened I'd straighten out or die tryin'.'

He meant every word — and could see she believed him now. She dashed a tear from her eye and managed a smile. 'I'll be waiting, Lee,' she whispered fervently. 'I-I reckon we'll have a lot to talk over when this nightmare is behind us. Don't you?'

Lee Kirby could only nod wonderingly as she turned and left. He'd been afraid to think how she might react when she realized just who and what he was, for it had been during his long,

165

caged hours that he'd finally realized he loved her.

The thought of old Moss beating his way for Macallister hurried him along as he worked Joe Rolfe's gadget into the lock. He knew he was reluctant to quit Macallister and leave it to the trouble which he had helped create, yet decided he could only face up to that once he was free.

Sweat burst out on his forehead as he jiggled and twisted without result. He heard the town clock chime the quarter-hour. Further endless minutes of feverish failure ticked by. Maybe Joe should have sent a book of instructions?

Then suddenly the cell door was open.

He slumped for a moment, catching his breath, then was stepping outside.

The murmur of voices was distinguishable coming from the office as he legged it for the rear door. A quick tug of the draw-bolt, and then he was out in the night with the wind cooling his brow. He'd used up more time than he could maybe afford, but the important thing was that he was free and all in one piece. Thus far.

A couple of deep breaths and he went heading across the darkened yard. Stables stood at the rear but all were empty. He would have to 'borrow' a mount on his way to the Craig house on Mount Street.

He glanced back at the brooding bulk of the jail as he unlatched the gate. All remained quiet and his spirits were rising. He hoped it would be that long-nosed liveryman who discovered the empty cell. He had a good shock coming, that joker.

The laneway lay dark before him under the starlight. He headed off left but hadn't taken more than three long strides when he was halted by the sounds of rustling coming from a heavy hickory tree close by. The hair on the back of his neck lifted as he heard a voice hiss, 'Lee!'

He was about to break into a headlong dash when he realized he recognzed that voice. It belonged to Flint, Moss O'Shea's right-hand man.

The man's head and shoulders emerged from deeper shadows.

'Kirby? How in the sweet name of Judas did you get out? We was just on our way to spring you.'

It had taken Lee longer than he'd expected to pick the cell lock. He was beginning to wonder if he'd taken *too* long, when he glimpsed the unmistakable shape of Moss O'Shea in his hard-hitter hat detach from the dark outline of the shed in back of the tree and come towards them in the starlight.

'Howdy, Moss,' he said softly. He jerked a thumb in the direction of the jailhouse. 'They got careless and I got lucky. Where are the others?'

'Close by,' panted O'Shea, grinning toothily. 'Say, this is a lucky break, our not havin' to raise all sorts of hell bustin' you out, son. Now we can just concentrate on the silver. Damnit, I've been waitin' to get at that big dinero so long I swear I can taste it.'

'We'd best get the hell away from here,' Kirby put in, concealing his bitter disappointment. 'They are goin' to find that empty cell sooner or later . . . '

Without a word, O'Shea beckoned and scuttled off across the rear yard of the general store to reach the alley which stretched away towards the canting bulk of the old abandoned livery. As the trio approached the rear of the building, Kirby glimpsed the outline of horses with three figures standing by them.

'Get a good gander at this, boys,' O'Shea beamed as Tanner Hannigan and Rolfe joined them. He clapped Kirby's shoulder. 'Busted hisself out with no help from us. Didn't I always allow he had the real makin's?'

The three made grunts of agreement, yet Kirby reckoned he could sense Rolfe's disappointment.

The way he had it figured, Joe had wanted him to get clear away from Macallister. There was no doubt in his own mind that this was what he'd wanted also.

The sudden sound of a shout drifted to them from the direction of the jail. O'Shea barked an order and they mounted swiftly to follow the gloomy alley behind the main street as a full scale racket erupted.

'Lee's done busted out!' a distant voice hollered, and Moss O'Shea chuckled as deep as his liver. 'Tell us somethin' we don't know, pilgrim! I swear this is an omen, boys. This is our lucky night.' He hipped around in his saddle. 'Now, just where in hell is this mine, Lee?'

'Moss has decided we'll hit the mine and forget about the bank,' Rolfe breathed, riding close by Kirby's flank.

'They're welcome to whatever they got in the vault,' Moss declared magnanimously. 'I figured there'd be plenty hooraw and hoopla in town after we sprung you, so I decided we'd just concentrate on the mine. You claimed there's even more in there than in the bank anyways, as I recall?'

'Right,' Kirby grunted woodenly. Behind his blank pan, the man was furiously wondering how he might get to escape. And yet he had feared from the very moment he'd first heard Flint's voice that there *was* no way. O'Shea had waited too long and taken far too many risks to be fobbed off with any lame excuses for not delivering now.

Kirby felt he'd stepped out of one prison into another . . .

O'Shea signalled a halt upon reaching a stand of dark cypresses. The gang boss chuckled as he listened to the faint sounds drifting from the main street. Then he raised his hard-hitter hat to run fingers through his grizzled thatch — and his hard, humour-flicked gaze fixed upon Kirby.

'We'll be in Utah before they know what the hell hit 'em,' he announced. 'Which way is it, son?'

Kirby let a held breath go, aware of the tightness in his chest. He supposed he ought to be relieved they only wanted the mine. For that way at least, they might get to pull it off without killing anybody.

There was a brief slice of time spent thinking of Jade and how close they may have come to sharing something powerful together. Then he closed his mind to that thought, like slamming a door. There could be nothing for them after this night. Not a single damned thing!

He wondered if Jade would ever get to find out why he'd been unable to meet her . . .

He inclined his head towards the star-framed bulk of the squat hill beside the river.

'Down yonder,' he grunted, and led the way.

As they cleared the treeline and travelled in Indian file towards the creek, a man crept out from the trees then began to run off towards the town.

It said much for the stealth with which the O'Shea gang had entered the town that Ketch was the only member of the Booth bunch, who'd been prowling about in a futile search for Macallister's mine, to have sighted them.

But one was enough.

9

Just One Big Grave

The back-porch light threw Jade's shadow long behind her as she approached the house. She walked slowly, her manner reflecting her mood. She no longer believed Lee Kirby would show. Consulting her watch she saw that it was half an hour since the uproar in Trail Street which had marked Kirby's escape. Her father had rushed off to join in the search while she'd waited with a fiercely beating heart by the rear fence with two horses saddled and waiting.

She'd made up her mind to leave with him and go wherever he wanted.

She'd warned her father concerning the O'Shea bunch, and had tipped him off about the true identity of the smooth-faced Smith — without revealing how she'd come by such information. Yet Mitch Craig had still remained sceptical and had issued no special precautions. Jade felt unable to do more. So she'd waited on tenterhooks for the most exciting and uncertain hour of her life, ready to flee.

But he had not come.

Maybe he'd never intended to do so, she brooded. She preferred to think that than consider the possibility that he might have been hurt during his escape, perhaps even killed.

A neighbour had told her that the men at the jail had found the cell empty. She had to believe that he had managed to escape unharmed — and that the only reason he'd not come to her was because he didn't want to.

Another five minutes passed. Better unsaddle the horses and stable them again before her father returned. Funny, but she hadn't shed a single tear . . .

So she attended to the horses and returned to the house to pour herself a stiff shot. As she carried the glass on to the front porch, the tall figure of her father came through the front gate to make his slow way down the pathway.

'I heard the news, Dad,' she greeted, passing him the drink which he seemed to need sorely. 'Did he get clean away?'

'Looks like it,' the man sighed, dropping heavily into a chair. He pulled off his hat and leaned back. 'Don't know how he managed it and maybe we never will. But you know something, Jade? I reckon I'm right glad he broke out now. I sense I had grave doubts about his guilt, particularly in light of what you've told me about this Smith . . .'

He sipped his drink and studied her.

'Or what did you say his name was now? Not Smith . . . Booth wasn't it?'

'Solway Booth.'

'You still haven't told me where you came by this information, Jade. For that matter you've not revealed where you were half the day. I was concerned about you.'

'I'm too tired to talk, Dad. Let's just sit here and relax. It's been a very exhausting time . . . for everybody . . . '

With a grunt of agreement, Craig drained his glass, closed his eyes and folded his hands across his stomach. Studying his face, Jade realized that strain had cut deep lines in his face which had not been there before. He really must get a proper night's rest, she told herself. There had simply been too much excitement and upheaval for a man his age.

Yet the excitement was far from over . . .

Jade straightened sharply from the porch railing with her hand flying to her mouth as the muffled thunder of gunfire sounded from the direction of Crow Hill.

★   ★   ★

Coogan and Crean enjoyed their occasional stints with pick and shovel in the cool, lamplit galleries of the mine,

Coogan because he enjoyed physical labour in contrast to his sedentary job as clerk at the bank, and Crean because it gave him the chance to escape from the ubiquitous Mrs Crean . . .

The two were working steadily at the face, chipping quartz from the rock face and loading the pieces into the buggy. When the cart was filled they would trundle it back to the main gallery and stack it by the smelter. Their last attempt at operating the smelter had been a disaster, so they were now only required to dig and tote.

The buggy was soon full.

The workers set their tools aside, got behind the little vehicle and heaved their weight against it to send it trundling down the narrow rails. Upon reaching the smelter, they set about adding the contents to the pile alongside, after which they stole a tobacco break while squatting nonchalantly upon a pile of ingots that was worth more than they would earn in a lifetime.

The mine meant the difference between breadline and relative comfort for many in Macallister, and Coogan and Crean hoped it never played out.

Coogan raised his head at the sound of foosteps from the gallery.

'Race,' he tipped. 'Likely gettin' lonesome standin' watch up there all by hisself.'

Crean grunted in agreement. Nobody ever wanted to stand sentry except Race Thompson, the lazy liveryman, who usually spent most of his watch snoring. It was better to work. Standing guard was a boring job because nothing ever happened to break the monotony.

Or, hardly ever.

Things seemed anything but monotonous when Race Thompson from the stage company walked into the lamplit gallery holding both hands at shoulder level — trailed by six men holding guns.

Coogan simply gaped but Crean made a grab for his Colt. He froze at Moss O'Shea's shout: 'Touch that iron and you're dead meat, mister! C'mon, up with your dukes both of you!'

They obeyed smartly, and bulging eyes stretched even wider when they saw Kirby among the menacing bunch.

'I . . . I'm sorry, pards,' Kirby panted. 'They was on to me afore I knew anythin'. They . . . they knew the secret way in, so they did . . . '

'Craig showed the mine to Kirby,' Coogan accused bitterly. 'He must've been loco.'

'Shut your jaw, Coogan!' Kirby rapped, brandishing his .45. 'Well, Moss, did I steer you right or didn't I?' he grinned.

Moss O'Shea was wide-eyed with excitement as he hefted ingots from a sack. 'Rich, rich, rich!' he chanted, 'and I'd even move to have you made president when we git to Mexico. Come on, you saddle stiffs, grab some sacks and let's start loadin' up.'

As the outlaws set to work with a will, Kirby motioned the three workmen away from the smelter with his gun. He was moving them off towards the branch galleries until Hannigan realized what he was doing.

'What's goin' on, Kirby?' he rapped suspiciously.

'Hell, we don't want these here pilgrims raisin' hell before we're well gone,' Kirby replied. 'I aim to lock 'em in the explosives shack. All right, Moss?'

'Hell, I don't give a damn what you do with 'em,' came O'Shea's response as he bent to scoop up another slab of pure silver. Then as an afterthought, he added, 'Better go take a look-see outside while you're about it, pard. Just to be on the safe side.'

Kirby needed no second bidding. Full of brag and bluster at the outset, this first-time thief was suddenly shaking in his boots and leaking cold sweat as the reality of what he was doing hit home. All he wanted now was to be out of this echoing gallery, out of Crow Hill Mine — and to hell and gone out of Macallister.

Pronto.

The captives didn't fully understand what was happening as they were hustled along a lateral gallery, then were kept moving well beyond the explosives depot. Soon they were drawing close to the exit where Kirby's keen ear picked up the faint sound of boot leather grazing stone . . .

Reacting swiftly, he ushered his charges into the first gloomy recess, then held a silencing finger to his lips as he backed in after them. They stared at him uncomprehendingly, for nobody could figure what in hell he had in mind.

A handful of taut seconds later found them with far more to fret about as shadows angled into the main gallery and then four men in dark garb with guns in hand moved fully into their line of vision.

Kirby's scalp pulled tight upon glimpsing the smooth and dangerous face of Solway Booth. He pressed back against the prisoners as the outlaws paused to survey the spacious, high-walled work area ahead. Abruptly all cocked their heads at the sudden sounds of voices and laughter coming from deeper within the shaft.

'This way,' Booth said softly. 'Now, remember there's six of them against just the four of us, so we got to make sure we take them by surprise to make the most of the advantage. We'll give them one chance to drop their cutters . . . then we club them down. We don't want any shootin' to bring the whole lousy town down on us.'

Heads nodded grimly and Kirby sucked in a deep breath as the four padded onwards. Kirby could feel Coogan trembling at his side, had almost reached the bend in the gallery when a voice rolled up clearly from the lower depths. 'Hey, Kirby. What in hell's keepin' you?'

The four propped, puzzled. In the alcove, Kirby cursed under his breath. Flint called again. Lee could see by the expressions on the faces of Booth's men that they knew he wasn't with the main bunch. Their eyes darted this way and that. Any moment now they were certain to be sighted . . .

'Run for it!' he hissed.

His captives gaped uncomprehendingly. 'What?' panted Coogan. 'What in hell do you mean, Lee?'

'I mean, make a goddamn break for the mouth before the bloody lead starts to fly,' he hissed angrily.

'You're lettin' us go?' Crean wasn't able to comprehend this.

'You dumb sons of bitches!' Kirby breathed. 'Don't you understand plain English? Get while the goin's good. I'll keep them busy and occupied while you get clear. Now, *get!*'

They saw Booth's pince-nez flash as he swung his sleek head in their direction. 'We won't forget this, Lee,' promised Coogan. Then led the rush for the entrance as Booth's questing stare finally ferreted them out. 'Here goes nothin'!'

Kirby dropped to one knee as they

rushed away, the .45 in his fist whipping upwards to reach firing level and pump a fiery blast after the outlaws. The crash of the shot in the confined space made the .45 sound bigger than a howitzer.

Dust and rubble fell from above and four dark-garbed figures dived wildly for cover as the bullet clipped Booth's hat brim and whacked into the wall.

The outlaws triggered back but Kirby was relieved to see that the three towners appeared to have cleared the area unscathed. He rolled swiftly behind an outcropping and tucked his head in tightly as scorching lead whipped by, close and hot. There came a splintering crash and he looked up to see that one of the coal-oil lamps had been blown apart, the flames already licking over an oil-spattered stanchion.

Abruptly a second volley opened up somewhere beyond Booth's position and he glimpsed the silhouettes of O'Shea and Joe Rolfe opening fire upon the enemy from the rear.

Lightning fast and lithely, Ketch whirled in a blur and cut loose with a drumroll of fierce fire. Kirby felt something catch in his upper throat as he saw Joe Rolfe pitch headlong. Next instant, O'Shea was winged and forced to dive low behind a boulder. Then Hannigan, Flint and Tanner reached the battle zone and Kirby's fire chimed in with theirs to pin the Booth bunch down.

A wild flurry of bullets spanged and whined in Kirby's direction before there suddenly came a lull. Booth was too busy with the attack from in back to worry about him. His eyes cut to the entrance. He calculated it lay some sixty-seventy feet distant. Open ground with the help of a smidgen of luck and some mighty slick footwork.

But could he quit on his pards?

He felt bad as he ran a check list through his mind. Such as, were they really his friends? Joe Rolfe sure had been — but Joe was dead. Did he really owe Moss and the others anything? The honest answer had to be no.

Logic screamed at him to make a run for it while he still had the chance, but something stronger held him motionless. Maybe loyalty was stronger than anything else after all? Or maybe it was something much simpler that stayed his hand — like the urge to take out Solway Booth — surely a man who just had to die?

Then again, he brooded as he reloaded his .45, maybe he was simply too damned dumb not to know when to quit . . . ?

Suddenly, violently, Ketch was breaking cover and darting towards another ore cart further away from the O'Shea guns. The man zigged and zagged desperately but Kirby had him in his sights while he was still a good ten yards short of his objective.

He squeezed trigger.

Through roiling gunsmoke Ketch was to be seen somersaulting with his twin Colts spilling from his hands and arcing high as the final deep-throated sounds of death enveloped him.

Kirby barely had time to ascertain that the gunner was dead before two shots from the hulking Wannamaker snarled desperately close. He shifted position lightning fast but the next bullet scored his right thigh, shallow but painful.

Blasting back he heard an O'Shea man roaring at the top of leather lungs. He shifted position slightly, the smoke thickening every moment now. There was a staccato exchange from the left, then he distinctly heard Tanner's rasping bellow, 'The explosives are a-burnin'!'

Kirby felt his pectoral muscles tauten. In the heat of battle he'd forgotten that the explosives' shed stood close by, realized belatedly that the shattered lamp had caught alight within mere feet of the dynamite.

Instantly, whistling bullets became a secondary factor as true fear gripped every man in the Crow Hill Mine. Flames were already licking hungrily over the explosives' shed. Booth was first to break and run, followed closely by a bug-eyed Wannamaker with a limping Jackson swiftly overtaken by the fleet-footed Flint, and others outlined against the smoky haze behind as everybody made a wild rush for the entrance together.

Kirby, who'd set sail for safety the moment Booth cut and ran, covered distance like an athlete while ignoring the savage pain in his leg. Other dim figures followed. Every man there had his share of courage but the sudden risk of death by dynamite-blast had the bravest matching strides with the man with the widest yellow streak down his spine.

So they ran like the truly desperates they were — ran wildly for the beckoning mine mouth through flickering firelight and roiling columns of smoke. Suddenly they were running on air as flame kissed dynamite and the entire mine shaft blew apart like the barrel of an over-heated cannon . . .

Kirby felt himself spinning through the air but had no idea that the enormous thunderblast from behind had actually hurled him to safety through the mine entrance, until some deafening and uncomprehending time later he felt hands dragging him away. He turned his head to see the entire eastern façade of Crow Hill moving in a slow and grinding slide as thousands of tons of rock and earth shifted and shuddered to fill the man-made chambers . . . one vast pall of smoke rising against the blood-coloured moon.

He must have lost consciousness. The next thing he knew somebody was splashing cold water over his face. Shaking his head, he attempted to rise but lacked the strength. He was bleeding from ears, nose and mouth. He was deaf and dazed, and yet could now see clearly enough. Coogan, Crean and Thompson were hunkered down around him in the rocky creek bed, faces taut with concern.

The men were speaking but Kirby

couldn't hear. There was a grey fog edging the corners of his brain and he was immensely, brutally weary as he leaned back against Coogan's solid leg.

'The . . . others . . . ?' he croaked.

Heads shook silently. Kirby made to speak again, but it was beyond him. In the deepening silence he slipped into oblivion.

10

Marshals Come to Town

Jade Craig's light summer skirt swished prettily about her ankles as she came along the porch carrying a pitcher of lemonade. Kirby, in real need of something stronger, grimaced but wasn't about to complain.

Not now.

For, but for some solid good luck and a fast turn of speed, he likely would be down there with the rest of them by now — helping make up the biggest mass grave in the county.

'This'll buck you up, Lee.'

He lip-read her words as she poured a large glass full. The medico insisted he'd regain full hearing in time. The leg wound was deeper than first thought, but the physician and his 'nurse' appeared to be taking first-rate care of that also.

'Cheers,' Jade smiled, clinking their glasses together.

'Quick death,' he grunted, and forced some down. His eyes snapped wide with surprise. This 'lemonade' had bite.

He glanced up to see her smiling as she spoke the one word: 'Gin.'

He didn't have any trouble understanding that.

'Dad said you would need something to take the edge off the lemonade.'

'Your dad is a smart man. Where is he now?'

'He's gone to the jailhouse with the councillors, Lee. The marshals from Villanova have arrived.'

Kirby sighed and leaned back in the deep leather chair to gaze upon the rolling landscape beyond Crow Creek. Until now he'd been fully occupied with the simple matters of rest and recuperation. The Craigs had cared for him well and hadn't permitted anyone to bother him. Yet reality, in the form of the Villanova marshals, had already intruded and forced him to consider his future, or what there was left of it now.

Of course he could cut and run, he knew. Most likely he wouldn't get far in his present condition, but at least he might give it a try. Or maybe he could go throw himself on the mercy of the court by claiming he hadn't actually done anything illegal in company with the O'Shea gang . . .

A grim smile touched his mouth. Of course he'd do neither. He was too beat to run and too damn proud and stiff-necked to beg from anybody.

He'd simply sit here with his crossed boots resting upon the porch rail and wait for them to come drag him away. He was, after all, alive. Luckier than most.

A shadow crossed his features as he thought of Joe Rolfe. Joe was the only one he'd miss. He was a good man in a bad business. If he went to hell for his misdeeds, surely he wouldn't be lodged as far down as *hombres* like Booth or Fabian?

'Drink up, Lee.'

Jade's voice seemed to reach him faintly. He looked at her face and her expression was unreadable. Her attitude towards him since the mine blast had been friendly, attentive, yet curiously detached. He had no notion of how she felt towards him in the wake of violent events, although he felt reasonably sure she was glad he'd survived.

Maybe, like himself, she was waiting to see what would happen after the law got through with him.

He took another long pull on his glass, then closed his eyes, allowing the good sun to soak into his bones as he savoured the pleasures both of being alive and free for just a time longer. Drifting off, he was conscious of her nearby. She smelt of jasmine . . .

* * *

The sergeant marshal tweaked his moustache as he carefully studied the long and detailed report which his

195

junior officer had just finalized. Mayor Craig had supplied the bulk of the information for the report, and although Sergeant Clanton had been given a full verbal account of recent events in Macallister, he was still surprised by the length of the death list which the clerk had furnished.

The marshal ran his finger down the list of names and counted fifteen. Even by the violent standards of a federal peace officer, fifteen dead men over a ten-day period seemed unreasonably high.

Finishing off the report he set it aside and fiddled with his moustache some more as he studied Craig and his councillors seated directly across the jailhouse desk.

'A grim tally, Mayor Craig.'

'Surely. But all but four of them were outlaws, Marshal,' Craig felt compelled to point out.

'Yes indeed, surely no great loss. Booth and O'Shea were wanted for years. Viewed in a purely objective light, their fate would surely seem to have been a good thing. But a man can't help regret the innocent lives that were also lost.'

'At least the kinfolk of the dead will be well taken care of, Marshal,' Craig pointed out. 'We voted unanimously to use the last of our silver to form a pension fund for them.'

'Commendable — highly commendable, sir. I must say I'm quite amazed that you were able to mine silver successfully for so long and keep it a secret.'

'It might have avoided all the violence had we made it public.'

'Who can say?' the lawman responded. 'When do you intend starting work on the mine again?'

'We don't, Marshal,' Craig replied firmly. 'We've looked over that death list and now feel we've learned a lesson. No amount of wealth is worth even one dead man — let alone a tally like this. Not the way we look at it, in any case. The towners have voted unanimously not to reopen the Crow Hill Mine. And if we can rely on you gentlemen to make no further mention of it then nobody outside Macallister will ever know it existed.'

'Of course,' the sergeant said, rising. 'Now, as to the vacant post of sheriff . . . '

'Er, we already have one man in mind, Marshal,' Craig cut it. 'I can vouch he'll prove reliable.'

'I certainly hope so, sir. Your last sheriff was something of a disaster, wasn't he?' He paused. 'Now . . . what was his name again?' He consulted his death list. 'Ah, yes, Lee Kirby.'

Craig nodded. 'That's right. The late Lee Kirby.'

*　*　*

'You what?' Kirby gasped.

'Told them you'd died in the mine,' Craig replied with a grin. 'That was another unanimous vote we took at the citizens' meeting last night. We knew that the marshals would have arrested you if they found out you were alive. The consensus was that in saving the lives of Coogan, Crean and Thompson at the mine as well as contributing to the destruction of both gangs, you proved beyond any doubt you were no cold-blooded killer. Everyone feels you've earned your right to freedom, Lee. And freedom is here for you just for the taking — if you want it.'

'Oh, Dad!' Jade cried, bounding from the chair and throwing her arms about his neck. 'You're wonderful. You're all wonderful. Isn't that so, Lee?'

'Wonderful enough . . . I guess,' Kirby replied, a little stunned. 'You mean I'm really officially dead, Mitchell?'

'Yes. So, how does it feel?'

'I've never felt better. But, hell, I feel kind of beholden to you for that.'

'Well, if you really feel indebted, you can work it off in Macallister.'

'How?'

Craig dipped into a pocket and produced a five-pointed brass star which he dropped upon the supper table.

'We still need a lawman — and you're still the best-qualified man around, Lee.'

Kirby picked up the star. 'You mean you'd give me my job back despite all that's happened?'

'We believe we know exactly what we are doing. Well, what do you say?'

'Well, hell . . . I don't know . . . '

'He says yes.'

Both turned to look at Jade, who'd spoken. And in that moment the discipline the woman had imposed over her emotions during recent days was abruptly stripped away and the look she gave Kirby was as clear and unmistakable as anything he'd ever seen.

Finally he understood how she felt towards him. It was all he needed to know.

With fingers that were not quite steady, he pinned the star upon his shirt. And knew as clearly as he'd ever known anything, that he would never be taking it off again.

Other titles in the
Linford Western Library:

JAKE RAINS

Tony Masero

Cuba, 1898. When Jake Rains' best friend and fellow Rough Rider was fatally wounded, he promised to care for his widow — though Kitty Cartright's protector is Chris Leeward, owner of the L double E ranch. Jake arrives in Oakum and things look bad. There's trouble at the Cartright place, so Jake and his new friend, Sam, are determined to put things right. But as they face Leeward's band of vengeful mountain men, Jake must fight for his life.